T0017957

LOJMAN

"A parable of violence — of state mandation, of mothering alone, of being mothered, of the vastness of nature — that shocks the system like stepping out the front door into a snowstorm. What does it mean to be a woman, and to be mothered by women, who have suffered under such alienation? Ebru Ojen captures the experience of immense pain with dark fervor and deft lyricism."

— MAKENNA GOODMAN, AUTHOR OF *THE SHAME*

"I've never read anything like *Lojman*. Ebru Ojen doesn't shy away — or let her readers shy away — from the darkest human emotions, which she evokes in exquisite, excruciating detail. This intense and visceral story of an abandoned family and their descent into chaos will stay with me for a long time."

— HELEN PHILLIPS, AUTHOR OF *THE NEED*

"*Lojman* is a feverish account of the thrashings of an imprisoned body and soul and a hallucinatory examination of motherhood, individuality, and romantic love. A dark, original, exciting novel."

— AYŞEGÜL SAVAS, AUTHOR OF *WALKING ON THE CEILING*

"Ojen's willful characters know from the beginning that the landscape surrounding *Lojman* and the fates of its inhabitants are false images of nature projected onto them by the state and society. Their story defies all meanings assigned to the nature of motherhood, childhood, manhood by the languages that have constructed them. A compelling, excruciating, and sophisticated dissection of family as a house to which we're sentenced to love."

— NAZLI KOCA, AUTHOR OF *THE APPLICANT*

Lojman

EBRU OJEN

TRANSLATED FROM THE TURKISH
BY ARON AJI AND SELIN GÖKCESU

City Lights Books — San Francisco

Lojman © 2020 by Ebru Ojen
Translation © 2023 by Aron Aji and Selin Gökcesu
All Rights Reserved

First published as *Lojman* by Everest Yayinlari (Istanbul, 2020).

Cover photograph © Matthew King, birdsandbeesandblooms.com
Cover design by em dash
Text design by Patrick Barber

The poems quoted in this novel are by Fırat Demir, from his three collections
published in Turkey: *Yeni Cüret Çağı*, *Öte Geçeler*, and *Beyhude Kombat*.

Library of Congress Cataloging-in-Publication Data

Names: Ojen, Ebru, 1981– author. | Aji, Aron, 1960– translator. |
Gökcesu, Selin, translator.
Title: Lojman / by Ebru Ojen ; translated by Aron Aji and Selin Gökcesu.
Other titles: Lojman. English
Description: San Francisco, CA : City Lights Books, 2023.
Identifiers: LCCN 2022047867 | ISBN 9780872868984 (trade paperback)
Subjects: LCGFT: Domestic fiction. | Novels.
Classification: LCC PL248.O226 L6513 2023 | DDC 894/.3534—dc23/eng/20230127
LC record available at https://lccn.loc.gov/2022047867

City Lights Books are published at the City Lights Bookstore
261 Columbus Avenue, San Francisco, CA 94133
citylights.com

Sensin, sesin atlarımı korkuttu.

. . .

It's you, your voice startled my horses.

FIRAT DEMİR

LOJMAN

I

AMONG THE LAKES, THE DESIRE TO GROW INTO oceans. Silence, endlessly growing silence. The deep mountain craters! Lake Van stretching infinitely toward the yellow horizon, resisting change with its every drop, asserting its presence, vast and still, in tiny vibrations. Unlike those lakes that long ago surrendered to the desire to merge with other bodies of water, Lake Van streamed forth from dark desert caves, implacable and whole, spreading out like a mercury spill to merge with the horizon, suffusing the plains in its steam, holding the mallards, the lightning strikes, and the people in place.

The smell of sulfur wafts up from the soil, filling the air with an acrid mist from Mount Süphan to Lake Van, permeating the present.

Greenheaded and mottled mallards take wing from dry reedbeds and fly toward the valley near the village. Here they are again! Their feet brush the snowbanks on the plains. As the golden ring of the noon hour splits the sky in two, the mallards beat their wings on the horizon line and ascend among the dark clouds. For them, the village is an unfavorable destination. If at all possible, it's best to avoid the villagers altogether.

The reedbeds, the small hills are much safer. In fact, the villagers don't bother with these latecomers to the landscape, these ducks who steal into the valley in rows. Overcome by the routines of their daily lives, the people simply deal with the Erciş Plateau, as harsh and desolate as an arctic desert. They burn dry cowpats in their ovens and stoves, air out their barns, dig out their vats of herbed cheese, cook meals with the provisions left over from summertime. With detached industry, they live long lives in the triangle formed by Mount Süphan, Lake Van, and the Erciş Plateau. Into those lives, they fit reunions, separations, weddings, suicides, funerals, births, and murders. While life forever runs its course down below, the mallards, in search of rest, change their itinerary that usually extends from Iran to Russia; they glide from the Erciş Plateau to Çaldıran to spend the night among the reedbeds, in hot springs; they feed on insects and moss in misty nooks, and in the morning, they reappear over Lake Van as they descend to the plains. By day, they beat their wings, by night, they inhale the sulfur.

But mallards, just like humans, are subject to the senseless operations of happenstance. A momentary carelessness or inexperience can mean death in the span of a wingbeat. A stroll on the frozen lake can cause the ice to suddenly crack.

We cannot trust winter. Nature, though it allows for happy accidents, insists on disasters. If we are not attentive, it can easily bury our supposedly meaningful lives into history, like so much of nothing. When the burial is complete, the "important" life we once lived holds no meaning. We and everything we failed to make meaningful disappear in these unexpected encounters. The encounters, the missteps, and the detours are constant. We are not.

There is a time for everything. In nature's orchestra, the rhythm of wingbeats, the breath, and nature's melody must create their own harmony. If the mallard fails to take flight at the right moment and flounders, then its downy breast and webbed feet, wet from the hot springs, will become inescapably stuck on the icy surface. As planets revolve in their galaxies with poetic rhythm, the motionless duck will surrender its body to the earth, as if settling on a new migratory path. And so here it is, another agonizing scene exalted before our eyes. Such scenes are always full of pain and heartbreak, and their beauty, at its core, belongs to nature's nightmarish darkness.

THE FINAL DAYS OF DECEMBER. ASIDE FROM THE MAL-lards spending time on the shores of Lake Van, nothing of note in the village. Winter had settled in, the time had arrived for fearsome storms. Frost penetrated the earth, the waters froze, the nights grew longer, the days shorter, leaving faint traces like tears rolling down dry, chapped cheeks. Everything was the same, as it was meant to be. Misty whirlpools, the sky's braided colors, the plains, the mountain, snow squalls, birches, poplars . . .

That night, it was as if all the snow in the world was falling onto the village, especially onto the gray lojman off in the distance, the teacher's house next to the elementary school. The darkness and the storm had joined hands, blowing whirlwinds ready to swallow that tiny dwelling, already nearly invisible in the snowfall covering the village streets with its pale blanket. The storm had piled walls of snow against the roofs, the doors, the cowsheds, clay ovens and troughs. The roads were closed, electricity was out. The howling from the mountain had grown louder, and the people withdrew to the furthest corners of their homes, waiting for the next day, for nature to relent.

In the East, the state builds its schools and the lodging for its teachers away from the residential areas of the villages. This lojman was no different, a forgotten dot on the village's suffocating landscape, distant and alone under the dark clouds. It looked out onto the plains through a thick fog that conjured the atmosphere of ghoulish tales. Fearsome winter monsters, jinn, dead donkeys, and poison trees had gathered at the darkest point of the night, laying siege to the little lojman, having sworn an oath to terrify anyone who dared to step outside.

Görkem knew very well how and where those sinister snow jinn, those armies of poisonous squalls hid themselves. She knew she would not be able to poke her head out that night, even if a great disaster were to befall her. Despite the restless thoughts sprouting in her mind, she knew she was still a child. And while she was happy to take advantage of the luxury of being a child, she resented Selma's indifference. Görkem hated that, when it came to her, Selma's all-seeing eyes were blind, becoming deep, dark, empty wells. Selma's sharp intellect stalled at the boundaries of her own existence, and her fingertips, usually so sensitive to the smallest vibration, turned to stone when they touched Görkem. Trapped in this cramped house perched on the edge of the vast plains stretching along the shores of Lake Van, she hated that she shared the same destiny with Selma, hated that she carried traces of Selma's blood in her veins. Selma embodied everything she abhorred. The darkest emotions in her compass pointed to Selma, and as she studied her crumpled figure, Görkem was spellbound, despite herself, by Selma's paralyzing pull on her. Staring at Selma's body slumped in a corner like a heap of broken toys, Görkem inspected her grimacing face, her usual indifference being shattered by physical suffering. It was fun to watch Selma wrestle with unbearable pain as invisible scalpels slashed at her belly, her loins, her overstretched skin.

Selma's contractions were becoming more frequent. Görkem couldn't tear her eyes away from her ankles, her calves. What large legs, she thought. The swelling had cracked Selma's skin here and there, turning her legs into hunks of diseased flesh. Görkem shuddered when her toes felt the warm, foul-smelling fluid that trickled from Selma's loins. She suppressed a gruesome groan of pleasure.

If Görkem hadn't known that Selma was giving birth, she would imagine that she was making love to Metin. Once, she had seen the two of them on top of each other in the bedroom and watched for minutes on end. Now, Selma was moaning with the exact same facial expression, the exact same movements. Görkem felt nauseous. How could she experience both pain and pleasure in the same way? Selma winced with alarming groans; her skin prickled with goosebumps, she shivered and shivered again, not from the cold but from anguish. The electricity was out. It was seldom on, so nothing seemed out of the ordinary now except for the baby being born. Everything was as dull, suffocating, and maddening as it always was.

CAUGHT IN LABOR PAINS, HER MOOD EVEN MORE CHO-leric than usual, Selma was screaming. Her cracking voice bore traces of an adolescent girl. That insufferable sound would get caught in a knot in her esophagus and, trying to force its way out, torment anyone in earshot. Collapsed in pain, Selma held out a razor blade and a pair of tweezers to Görkem. "Go to the kitchen, heat the razor on the burner, and bring it back," she said. At her command, Görkem's face faded like a sketch being roughly erased by a dissatisfied hand.

Once more Görkem realized how much she loathed Selma's imposing voice, always loud at trying times, and her hideous face that resembled something she couldn't quite put her finger on. She went to the kitchen knowing that she must follow Selma's orders to the letter, and she returned after heating the razor on the stove. The storm had picked up. It was as if the source of the howling was inside their very lojman, or more precisely, the gap between Selma's legs, spread open to give birth. Görkem was sick and tired of being there, of inhaling the foul air, and worse yet, of having to fulfill the woman's demands.

Will the baby be a boy or a girl? I wish it would never be born, wish its lungs were filled with poison instead of breath so I wouldn't have to struggle with such pointless questions, Görkem thought. If it had to be born, Görkem would prefer that it was a boy; if it were a girl, there would be no trace left of her own singularity. Selma was clenching her teeth. The vein that formed a thin line across her forehead widened, the skin on her face glowed as it stretched. One moment she broke out in a sweat, next she moaned, and in the end, unable to stand the pain anymore, she screamed again. The large drops of sweat trickling down her forehead and neck pinned Görkem's attention to the anguished face. Selma looked like a disgusting, watery soup. A soup that ruins feasts with its rancid, rotting flavor.

As her breathing quickened, Selma's face became even more intolerable. She kept pressing her enormous belly with her hands while spewing commands at Görkem.

"Go open the door!"

"It won't open," replied Görkem, her voice wavering in the air, "Selmaaa!"

"Stop crying, you're going to drop the razor."

On this cold day, on this wet and bloody ground, Selma's scolding felt even more unbearable.

Please let it be a boy, please!

Wonder what name they'll pick?

Enough, let the brat come out already!

"Go get Aunt Songül, hurry, or the baby and I are both going to die!"

This last sentence pleased Görkem. Quietly wishing that Selma would die before she uttered another sentence, she got up and walked toward the door. It would not open. Snow had piled up against it. Only Metin would have been strong enough to take on this icy giant. Besides, Görkem didn't like calling Songül 'aunt.' Still, she put her shoulder to the door and pushed with all her strength, but the door, immovable from the start, didn't budge.

"It won't open, Selma; I'm not strong enough."

They started crying. Selma, Murat, and her. A lovely choir. The thick whistling of the wind, the howling that rose from the void of the plains, accompanied them.

Selma's voice cut like a knife through the dirge.

"The candle is out. Go get a candle from the other room! And heat the razor again. The baby's coming!"

"Selma, if it keeps snowing, how is Metin going to come back?"

"All the way to hell that he went, it'll take him some time to get back."

She had never seen Selma this defeated. Normally she wouldn't say such things about Metin. Her pregnancy had robbed her of what miserly affection she bothered to show and had left her raw. This thing, how she wished it would die before it even stuck its head out of Selma's hole. The doors and the windows whistled. The only sounds missing were the cries of owls and wolves. Murat was wrapped up in the blue comforter; his crying had stopped, the tears had dried on his cheeks, and his snot had long since run down his chin. Unhappy about the new baby, he sat motionless and tense, staring balefully, stung by the idea of a new sibling joining the crushing grayness of the house.

Görkem's gaze was caught by the corner of the armchair. Despite its faded color, it seemed tempting, seductive. She was filled with an uncontrollable desire.

"Görkem, bring the razor. The baby's head is out."

Selma ruined anything beautiful. With her hideous, thick voice, her thorny, coarse hands, her feral eyes, she burned everything to the ground.

The baby, with bruised lips and a bloody head, managed to fling itself out of its mother's uterus within seconds. She hadn't expected such a speedy escape. In the blink of an eye, its shaky little hands, its wriggly body, and last, its feet came out of its mother. It must have been unbearable inside Selma's belly. Her body was like an elastic prison. It could stretch but never cracked open a door to freedom. Even if one escaped somehow, the elastic body would not relent; it bulged, it shrank, mercilessly reminding one of who was the master.

Selma grabbed the razor from Görkem's hand. She pressed it against the green cord coming out of the baby's belly and connecting to something mysterious inside her. In one deft motion, she slashed the cord. She took a piece of twine from her pocket and tied the end. Now, there were four of them in the dark lojman. Görkem beamed with pride from holding the baby before Selma could, noticing that its small body weighed as much as an adult cat. The baby was screaming mightily. So was Murat. A terrible duet. Two unripe voices. Still, preferable to the duet between her and Selma.

"What's its name going to be, Selma?"

"What does it matter, Görkem?" snapped Selma. After the hours of agony, she was in no mood to think of a name.

THE SNOW CONTINUED THE NEXT DAY WITHOUT
pause. From the depths of the sky, each snowflake carried the
darkness to earth, piece by piece. Görkem looked out the window and saw that the soccer field Metin and Yasin had toiled
to build last autumn was now completely buried in snow. The
crossbars of the goals were barely visible, their corners like two
little olives in the whiteness. No one would be able to play ball
before spring. Another reminder that she despised the snow and
everything that was cold. She felt goosebumps and pursed her
mouth as if she had swallowed something sour. No baby should
be born in the middle of winter, she thought. With her index
finger, she pried loose the putty hardening along the window-
pane. Adding her thumb into the effort, she tore off a piece,
rolled it into a ball, and played around with it for a while. Wary
of the vast landscape that left her feeling helpless, she pressed the
putty back in place and squeezed her body into the pile of cushions and blankets. She let her thoughts wander back to Teacher
Mahir who had been assigned to the village last fall. The image
of the young man entered her mind like the filmy smoke from
a snuffed candle. Her face lit up, a vague smile settled on the

11

corner of her lips. Would she ever see him again? It would be so hard to wait until spring. What a lovely face he had. The moment she saw him, she had noticed his deep dimples, his white teeth that shone when he smiled. The glow in his eyes and his perfectly even teeth gave him the power to get anything he wanted.

He had taught at the village for a few months, then vanished unexpectedly.

They said he had gone mad.

She heard from someone that he had butchered his mother. What a mighty human being! She fantasized at length about Teacher Mahir arriving through the thick snow. She pictured his perfect teeth sinking into his mother's flesh, the deepening grooves of his dimples, his mouth savagely taking possession of his mother's body as the snow invaded the plains from end to end. She decided that with his perfect features, the teacher resembled a fruit that only appeared on a hot summer day. She was overcome by a sudden desire to kiss him. She narrowed her lips, then she extended her tongue. A drop of saliva trickled from her mouth to her chin. Her stomach contracted from the disturbing, warm, sticky liquid as excitement came over her.

She imagined Teacher Mahir driving across the village, his hands on an imaginary steering wheel. She was surely in love with him. His image was so tempting. How she would have loved to place her ice-cold fingers in his armpits and warm them there. Only then would the infinite emptiness release her, even if just for a moment. She felt like a fish that can't swim, drifting in a sea of if-onlys. A lethargic creature, stumbling in the dark, hidden in the peculiar ocean of her brain. Odder than anyone could imagine...

"Selma, why did Teacher Mahir go mad?"

"You and your strange questions! Help me, I burned my hand."

SELMA HAD PLACED THE BABY'S DIAPERS IN BOILING water. The house reeked of bleach and steam. The washer had stopped working in the raging storms and the constant blackouts. The vapor emanating from the hot diapers reminded Görkem of her grandmother's house when they had visited last fall. It was like a bathhouse, saturated in steam. All its rooms smelled of bleach and old age. While thinking of her grandmother, she said out loud, "We still haven't come up with a name for the baby," and her voice was infected by her grandmother's sickly frailness. As if sensing this, Selma glared at Görkem. She kept her stern gaze on the small face that faded like a yarrow bloom in the evening light. Crushed under Selma's stare, Görkem resorted to studying the infant. Its face looked like a fresh peach; she thought the name Mahir would suit the baby very well.

For now, Selma's shallow attention was focused on the infant. She wouldn't be picking on Görkem and Murat, at least for the time being. Murat was in a pitiful state. He hadn't made a peep since the baby was born, watching both Selma and the infant with fearful eyes. He never said much to begin with, but now he was more cheerless than ever. Worse yet, he was starting to internalize the dreary atmosphere. Life with Selma necessitated this—living with death, decay, and cold . . .

THEY NEEDED TO PUT MORE FIREWOOD IN THE STOVE. Görkem and Murat were busy piling up old newspapers. Although the house was frigid, they were so utterly focused on what they were doing that feeling the cold didn't even occur to them. Selma hovered above them for a while, deciding which of them to task with lighting the woodstove; at last, she grabbed Görkem by the arm and practically dragged her over. She stacked a few pieces of firewood on her small, shaky lap. Lifting the stove's lid with the poker, she tapped on her daughter's shoulder a couple of times, reminding her to be careful. The gnarled brown bark was still wet, coming loose. Görkem's eyes lingered on the bark, which made her think of scabs peeling off from sores. The comforting smell of the wood filled her pink nose. She focussed on the next command she was expecting from Selma. She trusted her reflexes, accustomed as they were to enemy traps; she waited, on guard, her nerve endings sensitized. She could picture Selma's tongue rolling tensely inside her mouth, readying to bark the order to toss the firewood into the stove. When the order came, a sharp smell of ash spread through the house, licked Görkem's uneasy face, rose up in tufts, and

16

finally, submitting to the force of gravity that governs all things, sank back into the stove. She watched Selma throw in a piece of kerosene-soaked paper to ignite the wood. She realized Selma was burning paper torn from Murat's drawing pad. For a split second, Görkem almost reared up to stop her, only to be caught by her mother's gaze, which nailed her in place. The stench of bleach, hot steam, ash, wood, and kerosene filled the house, and they desperately needed to open the windows, but the weather was so cold and the snow came down with such violence that no one dared. They were prisoners of the winter's boundless wrath.

Darkness slumped on the plains like an exhausted, defeated father. The outline of Mount Süphan, obscured by the storm, was now completely erased; flocks of mallards had settled in the hot springs with quick wingbeats. And this is how two thirds of a winter day had passed them by. As the house quietly warmed up, the baby's murmuring rose through the silence, hovering above everything else. Selma was on the floor, on cushions stacked against one another. She was awake, even though her eyes were closed. Her hair was disheveled and damp, her face had sagged. The dried sweat that covered her body was bothering her. She folded her blistered fingers into her palms and prayed that sleep would come to her sooner than usual. Without it, she could no longer bear the deathly numbness.

She rolled her head to the side and glanced at the corner where she had just given birth. The room bore the traces of her arduous labor, blood and water splattered everywhere. The placenta she had torn from her body lay by the narrow wall between two doors. If she told Görkem to clean up the mess, she would disobey. By now Selma knew what would set off Görkem's pigheadedness, and she decided to avoid a fruitless fight. She checked the towel she had pressed into her crotch. There was some bleeding. She felt a slight pain in her ovaries. For a while, she stroked herself along the line that extended down from her navel. She moved her legs as much as she could. Her chest felt like it had been crushed under a pile of boulders.

She ran her weak fingers through her hair. Something about her needed cleaning. She needed to rid herself of the vulgar womanhood that clung to her body, she needed to find a book, read a poem. She moved her lips. *Who, then, picked this golden branch off the ground?* She had no strength left to recite or to read poetry. A strange feeling came over her. A strange feeling mixed with fear. But she longed to forget these sensations. Forget everything . . . The birth, the poems she'd read, her baby.

She stared at the ceiling. She drifted into watching it teem with figures that revealed themselves only to her. She tried to suppress her feelings, but something about her loneliness eluded her control. She braced her body to keep herself from crying. Poems seeped from deep in her mind; she began to mumble. *We are alone, not even a house near us, we are on our own, frightened.* From whence had this line materialized to unravel the knot in her chest? Her breath escaped her grip. She stopped resisting and released her body. Her lips, her chin contorted against her will, large tears began to roll from her eyes. She was crying so hard that her voice muffled the storm. After a while, she had completely exhausted herself, unable to move, her body overtaken by the soul of an old woman bewailing her sins.

She closed her swollen eyes. Her chest rising, sinking, she surrendered her body to gravity. As she thought about the children—their silence, their dispiritedness, which pricked all of her senses—the sleep she had long given up on stole into her windpipe. Turning into smoke, a creeping poison, it filled her body and took possession.

SNOW AND DARKNESS ROAMED THE STREETS, CACK-ling with manic laughter; winter's rule over the village and the lojman gained force with inexhaustible energy. The landscape became yet more vast with the howling that emanated from crevices in the rock, rabbit holes dug into the snow, and the mouths of clay ovens sitting outside the village homes. The world was hurtling toward infinity's end, and the only beings who resisted were the people. Rooted in earth that promised never to loosen its grip, they were caught in a melancholy inertia, waiting for the day they would unite with the soil and decay. Meanwhile, they continued to exhale their essence into the atmosphere, sending destructive vibrations into the universe, signaling their existence.

Selma stood before the window, holding up the candle to the glass, trying to make out the silhouette of someone she hoped to see outside. It took a while for her to realize that the image on the window was her own reflection. Dejected, she wished the storm would rip the lojman from its foundation and toss it into an infinite darkness. She had not fully recovered her strength. Her mind was muddled. A desire to disappear filled her heart to overflowing, taking hold of her entirely. If she could have her wish, neither the past nor the present would have meaning anymore. What a relief that would be! Storms, births, emptiness, Mount Süphan, flocks of mallards, frozen tobacco fields, the endless landscape before her eyes, Lake Van, all of it, all of it would disappear. She wanted nothing more but for the winter to swallow her up along with everything else. She pictured the distant poplar trees consumed by the darkness. Leafless, naked, they were far beyond her reach. The darkness began at the farthest tree and advanced all the way up to her nose at the glass, obliterating everything in between. She was next. Looking at her outline reflected on the window, she saw the threat and resigned herself to it. She moved slightly and noticed that her arm had wrapped itself around Görkem. She must have been next to her all this time. It seemed Görkem had snuck up on her, intruding on her privacy. She felt uneasy but let her arm rest on the small shoulders all the same. A high-voltage electric current flowed from Görkem to her. It was a staggering, unbearable sensation. Unable to stand the current much longer, she pressed her arm down onto the small body to force her to flee. Soon, she got what she wanted. The child freed herself and walked away.

She had completely lost any outward focus. The baby was lying in the middle of the living room and looking for a reason to fuss. Catching sight of this new creature lying on a broad cushion was like experiencing an unexpected act of violence. She froze in place—she had not been thinking about the baby. But there it was, stirring before her eyes, wriggling for its life like a worm cut in two. Appealing but also repulsive. Clearly, she was going to struggle to get used to its presence. She felt estranged, as if she had never given birth before. Had she felt this way with Görkem and Murat, too? She didn't know. Her memory hadn't retained a single image from their births. She looked at her baby again. This little no-name had already managed to put everyone on edge with its distinct personality, trying to claim a place for itself in the house. Especially Görkem. Selma had noticed it even before the baby was born. She sensed that Görkem didn't want to show any affection toward her sibling as she struggled to interpret things through the melancholy lens of her puberty. This creature was just a repulsive presence forcing Görkem to redefine the scope of her destiny. With the arrival of this new guest among them, whatever oneandonliness she had possessed was now dispersed like dandelion seeds, blown across the living room.

Selma's ears perked up for a moment. The baby's voice rose, shrill, bolstered by its gurgling. A complete alien in the realm of motherhood, she stared at the baby's face with a blank gaze; her desire to be free from all obligations had severed her from the creature she had brought to earth. She would rather drop dead than willingly offer her breast to that soft mouth. Still, taking a deep breath, she gathered her strength. Seized with nausea, she pushed her sore nipple into the baby's mouth, then holding its neck, she pressed the small body against her bosom. United with the breast, the baby suckled with dizzying delight and such powerful hunger that Selma couldn't bear it for long. Her stomach surrendered to the nausea. The tear in her throat grew into a giant cavity she couldn't control, and she started choking out vomit. The window's green curtains fluttered as if caught in a wind inside the house. The silhouette of Selma with the baby clutched to her breast melted in the fluttering green. The baby kept suckling, indifferent to Selma's retching. Disgust turning to pleasure, the deepest urges between mother and child rushed to the surface. The baby looked into Selma's eyes, as if inviting her to sin.

Selma was startled by the gaze of the creature barely larger than the palm of her hand. She couldn't tell whether those devious thoughts were products of her own mind or came from the baby's furtive gaze. Her legs trembled. She felt a thick, warm liquid trickle into her underwear. Her body shook violently. She was emptying. Reaching pleasure's end, she tore the baby from her breast and, protecting its small head, laid it down in bed. The baby stirred drowsily and soon drifted into sleep.

THE INHABITANTS OF THE VILLAGE WERE LONG asleep. The lojman had dug its claws into the plains, standing in the night, amid the deafening storm, with steely insistence. Selma was in the living room, seated at the table across from the window, squeezing her fingers, submerged in thought and ill at ease. Her thick locks fell over her face, hiding her mournful features. On the table were a few books, a yellow napkin holder, a half-full glass of tea, a teapot, an ashtray, a blue lighter, a pouch of tobacco, rolling papers, and a little ball of clay. All the objects looked forlorn, desperately waiting to be touched. She pinched off a piece of clay and closed her eyes in anticipation of the pleasure she would receive from this unusual food. She half opened her eyelids as she brought it to her mouth.

Hot water sweating off the teapot had pooled on the table. She squeezed the tobacco pouch with fleshy fingers that had become less swollen after childbirth. The pungent smell of the tobacco, moistened with apple peels, left a delectable sensation in her nose. Although she didn't feel like smoking, she couldn't resist its seductive aroma. With sluggish movements, she wrapped some tobacco in the rolling paper, bit off the edge of the paper with her teeth and licked the remaining surface with her tongue. She did everything with an attitude bordering on submission. She brought her masterpiece to her mouth, reached for the lighter with languid hands, and lit the cigarette, squinting her left eye. She inhaled the smoke, feeling her nasal cavity burn and the bitterness in her mouth intensify. Wearily, she released it. She had found a tiny hollow in time and wedged herself into it.

The harmonies inside her head grew louder. The gloom lifted, she loosened up. Even the messiness of the house, its coldness, seemed inviting to her; she was smiling. She wanted to savor the delightful emotions that lifted her off the floor, that tossed and turned her inside an emptiness. To savor the tobacco, the music from the imaginary orchestra, the lingering aftertaste of clay.

For some time, she enjoyed herself in her hollow, far from her thoughts; then, for some reason, she sensed that someone was walking around in the room, disturbing the emptiness with familiar footsteps. Now quicker, now slower. Rhythmically, as if dancing, one moment the footsteps moved toward the wall, next they approached Selma in her chair, next they stopped altogether. She was expelled from her hollow. The restful interval was gone, giving way to longing, uneasy desire. Sighing, she held in the breath that filled her lungs until she turned blue. This way, she could sense the steps more intently.

Without being warned, I'm nearing the spider.

The verse blended with the orchestral music, amplified, multiplied. She wanted to see the owner of the footsteps, to touch him. She had missed him, wanted to embrace him. She felt that, if she turned around, the emotions overpowering her body would vanish. Her eyes fixed on the floor, she couldn't bear the violence of the longing that scorched her. She knew who the steps belonged to, she yearned to writhe like a ball of mercury in her husband's palms.

Metin wasn't there. He had left days before the baby was born. Slammed the door behind him. Enraged, victim of a perpetual adolescence that could never rein in his volatile nature. The first few days, she hadn't minded Metin's absence much, she attached no importance to the situation, certain as she was that he would be back once his rage subsided. But more days went by, and she began thinking that this time, Metin was serious. Hiding her anxiety, she mentioned to Yasin that her husband hadn't been home in a few days. No need to worry, Yasin told her, Metin had probably gone into the town, and would be back as soon as the storm died down. As she listened to the footsteps, Selma's lips burned, then a searing longing spread over her skin that would not be satisfied even if Metin returned, held her, touched her. She tried to distract herself, to stop herself from imagining the worst. She looked at the random objects on the table, the blue lighter, the ashtray, the books, but none held her interest. Finally, her gaze settled on the little pool of water that had formed around the teapot. This tiny lake had so neatly marked its borders as it swelled; it was as lively and bright as the lush spring leaves that would fall and rot in autumn. She was taken by a desire to destroy that perfect ring that resisted the lethargy of everything else on the table, to smudge it all over the surface with her finger, to obliterate it. She pointed her finger at the small pool of water the way a needle defines its target before it pokes taut skin.

By simply existing on the table, the pool of water, a model of equilibrium, defied all the disarray of Selma's life and upset the course of her ever-weakening grasp on it.

Giving in to her unrelenting indecision, she withdrew her finger. The howling of the storm, torn from Mount Süphan and carried to the Erciş Plateau, reached her ears. With a devil-may-care gesture, before bringing her cigarette back to her lips, she tapped its long ash onto the water. The pool quivered with a sweet sizzle and dispersed.

THE NEXT DAY, THE STORM HAD ABATED. THE SKY was clear, a pure and pale blue. Rays of sun cut across the Erciş Plateau, casting shadows over the village. Mount Süphan, visible from the lojman's window, no longer looked like a hazy rock mass, but it was a real mountain, distinctive and grand with layers and layers of snow packed on its summit.

Selma stood outside. At last, she had managed to open the door. In the small dark hours of the morning she had swept the snow, shoveled some of it into piles. The air was icy, despite the bright sun. Today, she felt herself inexplicably capable and powerful. She might just become strong enough to take on any feat, strong enough to move giant mountains. She dwelled in the mania that gripped her, that gave meaning to her existence. Her radiant being overflowed, ready to inundate vast plains.

The winter had hardened everything. Lake Van had frozen over, even the water dripping from faucets had turned to ice. There was no water left in the house.

This tedious necessity had forced her to open the door to the outside in the morning frost and shovel snow in the bruising cold. Now, she was standing with her iron bucket in the middle of untouched, pristine snow, sucking on a piece of it. She had completed her excavation, found her motherlode, and tasted it. Now she could fill her bucket with fresh snow, melt it over the stove, do her housework and give Murat and Görkem a bath. Sorting all this in her mind, she slowly walked back inside. Her children sat around the stove like pups. She studied them with a frown. She stared first at Murat, then at Görkem for a long time. She considered their nimble fingers, all-seeing eyes, and quick intellects. Placing the bucket on the stove, she changed her mind about washing the children. She didn't have to. If they were cunning enough to enslave another human being, then they were strong enough to take care of themselves. Still, she could tell she was going to have a hard time silencing the rising voice of her conscience.

Her eyes locked upon the baby in front of the stove. She had washed it once since it was born. Now, she evaded questioning her indifference toward this fragile creature who would be lording over them for the next few years. Should she bathe it? Or should she let it fend for itself like the other two? So what if it was younger? Other people would say she was being cruel even for expecting Görkem and Murat to bathe themselves. She rubbed her hands together, deciding to leave everything aside and light the stove. The fire flared quickly and broke the cold, the house warmed up. She picked up the baby and washed it in the washbasin. After the bath was finished, she slumped down where she was, completely spent.

"WILL THE SNOWPLOW COME TO THE VILLAGE?" asked Görkem, disturbing the silence that had been building for hours. She was like a tactless, condescending guest. Selma had her eyes closed, her head resting against the wall. She merely sighed—a hint to Görkem that she did not care to answer a question that she found pointless.

Last winter, Metin had requested a bulldozer from the town to clear the roads. Görkem had been mesmerized by its dark yellow color, its magnificent body, and its jaws powerful enough to plunder everything in its path. She had seen that beautiful thing before, when they visited the township. Metin had told her what it was called, something that, if it were left up to Selma, she would not have learned for as long as she lived.

Once the roads were cleared, Metin would come back and clear the snow from the soccer field. Then he would organize a soccer tournament between the villages, and the whole village would turn into a carnival ground. Even if none of this would suffice to extinguish Selma's darkness, their world would still light up for a while. Görkem thought about all this while looking at the baby.

It didn't resemble any of them, even though it had already claimed a corner of the house like an uninvited visitor who expected to be fattened up. Strange face, too. Flat nose, eyes too close together, skin wrinkly and red. In their family, no one's nose, eyes, hands, or feet looked like that. The lips were very thin, too, the mouth wide. When crying, the mouth opened so wide that Görkem couldn't hide her astonishment. She asked Selma why the baby's mouth was so wide.

"Takes after your uncle, his was like that, too."

She kept thinking of her uncle's mouth over the course of the day. No matter how hard she tried, she couldn't picture his face. Finally, she asked Selma for the family album.

"Album? What album? I can't deal with that now," snapped Selma, shaking the book she was holding in frustration, looming over her with her usual, abrasive tone of voice, commanding her not to ask another question. Wounded by the scolding, Görkem took refuge in the only thought that made her happy, the image of Teacher Mahir. She dreamed of the two of them kissing, strolling from one end of the village to the other in the sunny days of summer.

She smiled as she imagined him in his unbuttoned, stained, faded shirt, his greasy hair, his hands bright red with his mother's blood. The image of those strong hands stained in her favorite color entranced her. Theirs was the most beautiful love on earth. As true and real as a hot summer day, a timeless masterpiece from the god who created wonders.

She couldn't wait to travel wherever the imaginary steering wheel would take them, his arm around her waist. She reveled in fantastic journeys across the skies, down to underground cities, up the mountain peaks, across the wide-open plains, into the blue depths of Lake Van. They would even fly into space, the glow of his eyes unfurling under the sun like two sunflowers. As the most splendid display of his madness, when they reached the ends of the stratosphere, Teacher Mahir would take his beautiful, bloody hands off the steering wheel, take her face in his palms, and inhale her smell as he reached for her lips.

Brimming with happiness, she puckered those lips that would instantly place a tiny kiss on Teacher Mahir's. Then another, and another. Then she latched onto his lips, bit into them until they bled.

She sucked on the blood from her lover's lips. As his blood flowed, her thirst became insatiable. Her tiny mouth expanded, like a hose sucking up sludge. She sucked on his blood with such an uncontrollable thirst that, in a matter of minutes, not a single drop was left in her lover's body. She had depleted him, transformed him, extinguished him. She was overcome by his shriveled complexion, by the smell of his skin mixed with the smell of his mother's corpse. The sight of him comforted her, calmed her heart, and she fell into a peaceful sleep.

SHE WAS LEANING AGAINST THE DINNER TABLE, HER fingertips examining her jacket carelessly tossed on the chair. She pinched its buttons, traced along its stitches. Where and how had she bought this jacket? How long had she been wearing it? How tattered it was. She could even see the dust particles aging on its surface. She picked up her phone, contemplating the fact that this jacket might have a longer lifespan than her own. Her reflection flickered on the phone's dark screen. How fragile the connection a person drowning in loneliness has to their own life, like the lines now appearing now disappearing on the screen. She wanted to call Metin, but there was no reception. It didn't seem possible that she could reach him with any device belonging to this world. With every passing minute, the distance between them was growing, the images of him vanishing from her mind moment by moment, like clouds slowly dissolving into the sky. The emptiness was thickening, congealing, snarling her body in its slimy, viscous matter, coiling around her arms and legs, leaving her motionless. A loud cry suddenly rising from the other room snapped her out of her thoughts; she flexed her body as if coming out of a thaw and headed to the bedroom.

She lifted the baby in the air, holding the fresh face at eye-level. Shiny eyes, toothless mouth, cute, squirming like a bug. She looked at this creature that had ripped all her strength from her, disturbed her chemistry, plundered her minerals, and come into existence by practically destroying her. What a powerful gaze! This willful face of a spry old man seemed to intimate the existence of something more significant than itself. It had wrested what rightfully belonged to it from the one who gave birth to it. The baby didn't have a name yet. Everything she had created with her husband, including this nameless, dark being pushed her away from love. Because of the children, no trace of passion was left between them. It was only when she turned her back to the things they had created together that she felt closer to Metin, more in love with him.

She was seized with a desire to slam her baby against the wall and kill it. But she knew she wouldn't. She couldn't kill it. This nameless, small creature had stripped her of exactly this: her glorious self-confidence, her power to destroy. A product of nature, she had to live by unnatural laws. She lacked the self-confidence of the alligator mother who killed and ate her offspring. Her children had hacked at her courage, ripped her from her true origin to bind her to the arteries of life.

Her body was trapped somewhere alien to herself, by something she could not give meaning to. Suffocating in its arbitrary chokeholds, she could not figure out what to do against its powerful force. She felt like a shipwreck lodged in the deep, dark seafloor. Caught in the tides of her thoughts, watching her life force wither, she pressed the baby to her bosom so she wouldn't have to hear its voice, and fell into a crying spell.

34

WHEN SHE AWOKE IN THE EARLY MORNING HOURS, she sensed that the usual irritating atmosphere of the lojman had changed. Selma's voice came from the living room, chirping with happiness. She was strangely joyful. The smell of fried potatoes filled the room. The stove was blazing. Although she was a coffee addict, she had brewed tea instead. The house had been cleaned, the furniture in the living room rearranged. Dance music was playing on the computer. Songs that reflected Selma's inimitable bad taste played in random order, with slow, melancholy numbers followed by cheery dance tunes. She had put on a pair of red bell-bottoms that fit perfectly tight over her hips, and a velvety blue blouse that accentuated her breasts. She had swiped mascara on her lashes, colored her cheeks with blush. She had put on huge earrings and adorned each finger with a different ring. She hurried back and forth through the house with quick boisterous steps.

Görkem was used to these unhinged outbursts of Selma's sickening, misplaced artistic spirit. But even though she hated Selma when she was in this mood, she didn't hesitate to reap the fruits of these joyous explosions that occurred so rarely. She ran about with Selma, they were like two mad cows in the house, now fetching food from the kitchen, now tidying up here or there. Murat had woken up before Görkem, and was trying to keep up with his mother's exuberance. He hovered above his sibling who was only a week old, trying to play with it, despite its flustered whining.

The sunlight coming through the window wasn't sufficient to light up the room, but it gave the house a cozy feel, making the tiny dust particles floating in the air shimmer. Görkem kept blowing on the dust particles, setting them in rapid motion, finding a way to amuse herself while the breakfast was being prepared. The dust recalled the images of star formations she had seen in encyclopedias, countless particles that arranged themselves into mysterious, orderly designs. For the first time in a long while, the lojman felt bearable. That gloomy, soul-wrenching atmosphere was gone, replaced by the carefree happiness of ordinary families.

During breakfast, Görkem did not let her guard down, knowing that Selma's unanticipated bliss could turn into a fit of anger at any minute. Someone who had just torn another being out of her body and flung it into the world, shouldn't she be exhausted? Selma looked neither tired nor weak. Nevertheless, there were foreboding notes lurking in the aura of her energy. She resembled a racehorse that had gathered up all its strength for its final race and would die once it was over. She had never shown any intention to reconcile with anything in her life. She was divorced from everything, including herself.

When she didn't actively hate Selma, Görkem was simply tired of her. No matter how hard she tried, she could never accept that she was Selma's child. It had to be a mistake. A mistake or an irreversible accident.

She was as certain of Selma's complete lack of love as she was of her own. She despised the clothes Selma wore, the way she talked, the poems she was always reading and trying to memorize, and beyond all that, her crudeness. Her demeanor toward Metin was so artificial that Görkem could barely keep herself from laughing every time she witnessed it. And then, using pregnancy as her excuse, she had become more overbearing than ever. If she had to give birth to get attention, Selma would give birth. And, there: she had done it again.

THE FIRST LIGHT OF MORNING. THE ABSENT-MINDED
expression on her face, her languid gaze, the deep lines between
her brows like irreparable cracks in a wall. She had fallen asleep
in the narrow armchair. She hadn't even thought of covering
herself; she was scrunched up like a shriveled, singed plastic bag.
It had not been a good night. She was 42 years old, and this
morning she felt no benefit from her maturity.

She frowned. She had never liked the morning sun. Always
afraid that it would blind her, she would grimace when the first
rays hit her face. Now she tried to endure it for a few moments,
but she couldn't. Annoyed, she stood up. Her neck was stiff, her
arms were numb. She held her head in her hands and grew even
more annoyed when she realized that she had difficulty turning it sideways. She placed her hands on the wall and tried to
stretch her back like a cat. At the foot of the armchair, she saw
the newborn asleep on the floor and marveled that she hadn't
crushed it when she stood up. The baby was slowly beginning to
wake up. She watched as its beguiling stirrings gradually turned
into cheerful hand and arm gestures. Soon it would signal its
hunger. She couldn't bear to look at it, she didn't want to feed

it. She straightened her body with a sigh. The pain in her neck was unbearable. She picked up the baby, who fell back asleep instantly, and laying it next to Görkem she got into bed along with them, pulling the covers over her head. From a small opening, she watched Görkem's face: rosy, buoyant as cotton candy.

Foolish girl, she thought, clueless about her wretched life. A lock or two of her red, curly hair cascaded down the pillow in ringlets like dormant tornados. She wondered why a head of curls like that had been assigned to such a lovely, thoughtful face. How could this little girl with the curly hair and short neck belong to her? It seemed like someone was playing a trick on her.

Her children were parasites! They were nothing but maggots that had first depleted her calcium deposits, then plundered the most sensitive parts of her soul to take them as their own, pinning the features of her body onto theirs. One had stolen her smile, one her high cheekbones, one her expressive gaze, one her skillful hands, one her shred of hope, one the shape of her eyes, and one her passion for poetry. What's more, one took the space between her genitals and her navel, one her curly hair, one her even teeth, one her increasingly shrill laugh, one her imposing tone of voice, one her anti-romanticism, one her belief in the coming apocalypse, one her hand gestures, one her jealous kisses, one her indescribable singularity, one her discriminating taste, one her self-composure, one her large eyes, one her tilted head, one the healthy functioning of her pancreas, and now, they wandered about like fresh, green, creeping vines, still searching with starved eyes for anything more they could take from her. If there is any proof to convince me that these excreting bodies have come from mine, show it to me! Show me the truth. Prove that I'm a prisoner with a life sentence. Whoever it is that claims children are adorable should stop lying.

She hated all that nonsense about the mother who would die for the sake of her children. For her, everything people had ever said about motherhood crumbled to pieces, like a building with no foundation collapsing at the slightest tremor.

Her face quivered. The sweet, nauseating smells of her children joined forces, and rushing through her nostrils pressed against her brain. She swallowed air to tamp down the bile that rose from her stomach. Her heart was pounding, her eyes flickered. She groaned, her chest heaved. She could almost foam at the mouth.

She sat up, jolted by the wave of hatred. She didn't want to look at her children lying in bed. As she got up to go to the living room, she felt a little dizzy. The living room had received its share of yesterday's cheerfulness and looked like a battlefield. A few books lay open on the table, though they looked like they hadn't been read. The carpet was dotted with red and brown stains of unidentifiable origin. The same stains were on the floorboards. When she noticed the dessicated cactus on the bookshelf, she was seized with the illusion that she had been away from home for a long time.

Patiently, she examined the gray walls and gray ceiling of the lojman. The repulsive structure suffocated her more than anything, as if the roots of every kind of evil penetrated into these buildings. Ever since they had married, she and Metin had gone from one state-sponsored teacher's house to the next. With each new shade of gray, she felt more imprisoned, became more ordinary.

Her gaze lingered on Murat, who slept curled up on an armchair. How much he resembled her husband. Metin had bequeathed his childhood and then deserted them. Oh, to strangle him now so he doesn't grow!

SHE OPENED THE DOOR. BUTTONING UP THE COAT she'd thrown on at the last minute, she wrapped her face and neck tightly with her scarf and put her hands in her pockets. The moment she set one foot out, she realized that the storm was even more violent than she'd expected, which upset her. She pulled out her cell phone—no reception. Still, she flicked to her messages. Wrote and wrote, then deleted. She was wary of being alone outside, left to the fierce howling, the stinging winds, twisting inside an endless moment, becoming more ensnared as she struggled to break free.

She was drawn to the trees, their branches, everything that didn't belong to the sky. The cold blast rising from the Erciş Plateau formed whirlwinds, the poplars shook, trying to withstand the winter. The soda smell rising from Lake Van reached all the way to her nose; she shuddered. Alert to the howling in the distance, her consciousness settled into her body. Her eyes retreated deep into their sockets.

Something moving toward her caught her attention. It approached, taking the shape of a body. Soon the steps grew audible, leaving behind tracks, rustling, and patter. She squinted; as the body closed in, she recognized the familiar face.

"No news?"

"None."

"I have to raise the flag tomorrow, Selma Hanım. You can't do it on your own, I'll come and raise it."

"Okay."

"I seem to have kept the school key; you should keep it, Selma Hanım, and I'll get it from you tomorrow."

"...."

Anger rippled across her face. Reluctantly taking the key, she walked away without saying anything else.

Back inside the house, she looked frozen. Görkem met her with questioning eyes, large with apprehension.

"Where were you?"

She didn't reply. The lojman was frigid, the stove completely out. Murat was standing in the middle of the living room with the baby cradled in his arms.

"Were you kids cold?"

The blistering wind had flushed Selma's face. The children looked at her, inquisitive, hungry, and cold. Even the newborn had the stare of a judge. Faced with the expectations of her children, she felt like a piece of meat surrounded by carnivorous fish. She quickly pulled herself together, brushed away any disquieting thought remaining in her head, and made a mental list of tasks. First they had to heat the house. She and Görkem attended to the stove together. Next, she prepared something to eat. Between chores, she nursed the baby. After tidying the house, she suggested that they watch TV, but there was no electricity. When the children didn't complain, she decided to pop some corn to make it up to them. She went back to the kitchen, to the pots and pans and cutlery. In the chaos of the kitchen, she tried not to fall prey to her mind. She gathered the dirty plates, wiped the counter, the stovetop, made sure she placed everything back in the cabinets. The fussy babble reached her ear. She was again seized with frustration by the reminder that the baby had to be fed frequently. The brief sense of peace she'd enjoyed while cleaning the kitchen quickly disappeared. She was furious that the baby picked inopportune moments to remind her that it had to be fed. How much longer could she endure these cries! Giving birth was an ugly sham. One more creature in the world who snatched everything she had from her: that was the result and nothing else.

Where in hell was Metin? Why had he not returned by now? He had to come back right away and save her from this chaos. Anxiously, she turned to Görkem.

"What is the date today, Görkem?"

"26th," she said, checking the calendar.

"Your father has been gone for exactly two weeks."

"Who will raise the flag tomorrow, then? Will Yasin come and raise it?"

"Yes, we spoke. He'll come first thing in the morning."

THE EVENING TWILIGHT SPREAD SLOWLY OVER THE plains. The hawthorn trees, the poplars, still gave the impression that winter had never arrived in the village. Mount Süphan, ever-imposing, had moved from the sunny side to the shady side of its day; it looked calm, imperturbable. The winter stream flowing through the plains, the dirt paths stretching to the beet fields, the haystacks left from autumn were all in harmony. The simple hues of evening softened the sounds of winter, extracting notes from its noisy clamor and handing them off to a delightful orchestra.

The greenheads flew down from the slopes of Mount Süphan, leaving behind the snow-covered cliffs where they'd been resting into the late hours of the afternoon before beating their wings toward the hot springs below. Once they descended into the reedbeds, no sign would be left of them.

A winter fly was tracing compass-perfect circles near the ceiling, its shadow skimming across Selma's face. She looked like a toy with a dead battery. She felt as if she'd just been told that soon her childhood would be completely erased from her memory, and she was still in shock. "If I am to forget everything, what is the point of all this?" she asked, thinking of the mallards, of Mount Süphan. She leaned her head back. A knot settled in her throat, one that could easily be undone if she could only cry. She could neither focus her eyes nor clear her head. Listening to her heartbeat, she tried pacing her breathing to subdue the machinery that refused to cool down. The sounds of children playing outside rang in her ears. How on earth could they venture outdoors at this hour, she wondered? Still, their happy sounds cheered her up. But soon enough, nasty thoughts assaulted her once again. In the old days, children were kidnapped. Murdered. Did that not happen anymore? Or, did all the evil in the world vibrate at a frequency only children could sense? This sentence was absurd, like the ones before. She pressed her brow to the window. Nothing was visible apart from the vast, boundless darkness. The children's squeals tore the sheet of silence in two and bent time. They flung her into the past and then back to the present. She remained suspended in the present. Had she fed her children? Had she nursed the baby? She sighed, looked first at her daughter and then at her son, who had come back inside. Murat was listening intently. Görkem was describing a memory mixed with lies.

"So we went after them, running. My dad caught that thief right away, beat him up. He was much stronger than the thief, much bigger too. The thief was begging my dad. But my dad wasn't persuaded, he brought him to the police."

"Your dad would never beat anyone, or turn anyone in to the police," roared Selma.

46

Hatred and a touch of shame flared on Görkem's face. Would there ever be a story, a day, a moment, uninterrupted by this woman's shrill voice? Her cheeks flushed, she tugged on Murat's cardigan to change the subject.

"Why did you lose the wheels of the truck I gave you?"

COME WHAT MAY, ONE DAY, I'M GOING TO KILL myself! Once this thought settled in her head, the person that had been split in two became whole again, and she saw herself exalted in her own eyes, she felt herself rising above everything else. Sitting in the armchair with a book in her hand, she dreamt of the time, someday in the near future, when the exquisite torment, the existential agony would end. She breathed in and out, as if intoxicated by a captivating scent. Her field of vision became clouded by mists that melted away as they touched her body, water droplets evaporating. The taste of despair knotted in her throat. Yet, what an exultant feeling it was to contemplate death like that. No experience in life could ever compare to the pleasure she derived from this wondrous thought. No other idea could ever render her so powerless, nor could she ever submit so willingly to anything else.

In an ecstatic swoon, her body slid from the armchair to the floor. She touched the objects in front of her and tried to tidy the disarray. The orderly movements of her hands calmed her nerves. She pressed her nails into her flesh. No matter how hard she tried to forget, the idea of suicide beckoned, appearing before her again and again, raising its head from the tar pits, bounding over ditches, sprouting in the most unlikely circumstances. She was aware that her will to live was slowly vanishing into the vast landscape. Yet, inexplicably, she was able to resist the attraction of losing herself in the moment, obstinately holding onto a present that portended evil.

She was weary of the world she inhabited. The feeling of emptiness, of impotence, had exhausted her. The knowledge that she could never defeat the invisible guard who kept her in chains, that she could never pierce through the suffocating, stinging orb that encircled her body, causing her unbearable pain.

Those people who insisted on taking trips even though they were condemned to return to the same inert landcape aroused in her a revulsion mixed with envy. A friend who had lost his wife to an uncurable illness last year had finally given up traveling to stay put. The Philippines, the Maldives ... he would travel to places with names that ended with the plural suffix, praising their beauty, knowing full well that Selma hated comparisons. "Good thing she died and was finally rid of him," she said aloud. She liked the voice that came out of her mouth. Bringing her hand to her lips, she wanted to catch the self-satisfied, resolute voice bent on death. She moved her fingers along her teeth, her lips. Her relationship with her body had been better before she fell into the gruesome pit of love for another person. She used to run her hands all over her body without inhibition. Now she was a hopeless case who had abandoned everything that stirred in her, everything alive and human.

She stood up. She took her notebook from the bookshelf. Licking the tip of her index finger, she flipped through the pages until she found a list. With a pencil, she went over some of the items on the list. She stopped at one, saying, "Another line erased," and put the notebook back.

The lojman shook like it was being whipped in a butter churn. While from inside the house the night wind felt violent, she could hear it quietly licking the Erciş Plateau, the poplars holding onto their roots, the rabbits drawing curlicues on the snow. As the house sank back into silence, everything became shrouded in darkness, desolate. Overcome by sleep at last, the children lay unconscious, unmoving.

The baby had cried itself to sleep, not having had enough to eat. Görkem and Murat had both pulled their knees in, like two synchronized gymnasts frozen in midair. This image proved that everything, like night and day, held its opposite in its embrace. The two were nothing like each other, she mused. Their looks and their personalities were completely at odds. In truth, she was aware that she didn't know her children very well, and she didn't think she had to.

Görkem had always struck her as a stubborn, scheming person. The moment she was born, Selma knew she was always going to struggle to understand her. She had such a mercurial, striking temperament. From the start, it was clear that Görkem would weigh heavily upon her. She was a monster who always demanded more of everything: food, love, anger, forgiveness, enmity. For a while, she had relished having given birth to a person so unlike herself. Then, everything changed; an insurmountable rift, a haggling spirit, a profound animosity formed between them. She was so sick of Görkem's questioning, reprimanding gaze that at times she found it hard not to tell her to just get up and leave. The fact that Görkem was a child shouldn't stand in the way of cutting her loose. But then there they were, other people and their bellyaching. All that idle chatter, the barrage of incessant rebuke and accusations. Righteousness! Hyperbolic, fabricated subplots that made her into a monster. Talk, talk . . .

As she continued to brood, the capillaries in her brain were exploding, ready to dissolve into infinitesimal particles and scatter over the world.

IN THE BLIND HOUR BEFORE MORNING, SHE WOKE UP to a knock at the door. Lifting her head off the pillow took serious effort. Her face was in disarray, flattened by the cold, her expression frozen. As she slipped from under the covers, her body came in contact with the frigid air. It was a dreadful sensation. She was suddenly flooded with a desire to cry, she wanted to scream. The never-ending cold had taken hold of her life. She wanted to free herself from this feeling, from the cold, from the darkness, from her life.

Murat's thin, lilting voice cut through the cold and reached her bed.

"M-o-o-o-mm-y! Uncle Yasin is here."

Next came Görkem's high, adolescent voice. "Yasin is here, Selmaaaa!"

Had the bedroom walls collapsed on her, she wouldn't have felt this desperate. The dread of having to see anyone gripped her heart. Her skin bristled, she jabbed her tongue with her teeth. Her children's voices irked her so much that she barely kept herself from throttling them. Her eyes fixed on the ceiling, she inhaled and exhaled until she couldn't breathe anymore. She didn't want to do anything. Why did the flag have to be raised? Who cared about this in the middle of a doomsday snowstorm? Everything was meaningless, exceedingly so. She'd have to get out of bed, change clothes, step on the cold concrete, see her children's faces, wrestle with their endless demands, make it to the cabinet at the other end of the house, take out the flag, open the icy door, let the frigid air hit her face, and as if all that weren't enough, she'd deliver Yasin a grateful smile in return for his nauseating favor. Just the thought of it made her shudder. If only Metin were here. He would manage all this nonsense and tidy up the entire mess. Metin was a multifunctional machine that cleared the inside of the house, the inside of her head, the inside of her stomach, and now, like a sudden malfunction, he had disappeared.

She brought Metin's face before her eyes. For a moment she was filled with the desire to frolic with him under the sky, across the meadows. She imagined the sun gently warming their faces, holding and squeezing Metin's clever hands, the two of them watching the clouds in the sky moving independently of one another. A fresh wave of excitement filled her. She pursed her lips and closed her eyes, wanting to lock in and seal off that sensation somewhere in her mind so she wouldn't forget. For a time, she remained still, her lips pursed, her eyes shut tight. Then, she pulled herself together and let go of her dream.

The cabinet was just the same as the rest of the lojman. Worse than the cold, only good for reminding one of bad memories. The flag was in the cabinet, folded neatly. Before handing it over to Yasin, she stared at it with blank, empty eyes. She was tempted to wrap that fabric always reeking of naphthalene around her head and smother herself. The sharp smell settled into her nose. She wanted someone to hurl her kilometers away. After a minute, a hand touched her wrist. In response, she let the reeking flag slip from her hands. Her eyes met Yasin's.

"Are you alright, Selma Hanım?"

He looked at the children from the corner of his eye. He had sensed that some things weren't going well in the house.

Caught in Yasin's gaze, Selma lost her temper. She wanted to tell him whatever came out of her mouth, upbraid him, insult him, gouge those kindly eyes with her nails. Yasin was an otherworldly creature that could be destroyed only by another life form from outer space. His voice robotic, metallic, sexless, he was like a computer with a human body.

Flashing in his eyes were texts that questioned her humanity.

Are you real, Selma Hanım?

What is real, Selma Hanım, is it you?

Is it really you, Selma Hanım?

"Still no news of our teacher?"

"…."

"Whether the roads are cleared or not, tomorrow I'm going to take Recep with me and go to the township to ask about Metin. Don't you worry, Selma Hanım." The howling in the distance blurred Yasin's voice. Should she thank him for planning to go to the township? For putting up the flag, for keeping an eye on them, for reminding her of the things she had to do? Who had asked him to do all this, anyway, who had called on him? Who had let Yasin into her life? The stupid man meddled in everything, as if it was a privilege he had earned. She was angry at Metin for encouraging such audacity.

She frowned. All this nonsense had to end right now. She noticed a nearby shovel with a black handle. An irrepressible vision appeared before her eyes, in which she hit Yasin on the head with the shovel over and over, smashing his skull until his brains spilled. Still not satisfied, she stomped on the blood-splattered pieces of flesh. Then she gathered Görkem, Murat, and the baby. She swung the shovel at their heads. The three skulls cracked in one blow, blood splashing over the walls, the hallway, her clothes. Her face glowed with the light of madness. The satisfied look in her eyes matched the smile that appeared at the corner of her lips.

"I should be going, Selma Hanım."

The wind had swept snow into the lojman and made the frigid air inside feel even colder. She shut the door, which sounded a depressing wheeze as it closed. She went to the living room, her steps small and reluctant. Ordering the children back to bed, she took the baby from Murat's arms and went into the bedroom. She stared at the baby's mouth searching for the nipple, the scrawny fingers resembling insect legs. She didn't want to nurse the baby. But her unwillingness could starve the poor thing to death. She brought her breast to the small, soft mouth. She turned toward the window to keep from looking at the baby. Yasin was outside, surrounded by snow drifts, struggling to raise the flag on its ludicrous pole. Tears began streaming from her eyes. Things she couldn't withstand kept multiplying, and the harder she tried to resist, the harder they charged at her. She was suffocating. She hated that she was unable to split these parasitic reptiles' heads from their bodies. When had she become so submissive? When did she lose the strength to hold at bay the very thing that forced her into submission? She couldn't bear this thought.

With all her being, with everything that made her Selma, once again, she had lost. Defeated by her enemies. By the lojman, by the children, by Yasin.

NOON ALREADY. IN THE VIOLENT WIND, THE FLAG had wrapped itself around the pole and frozen onto the metal as if it had never been raised in the first place. The storm had piled heaps of snow on the steps of the lojman, the door was practically invisible. Görkem tried to wake her mother from her deep slumber. If Selma insisted on not waking up, she would faint from hunger. She threw her skinny arms around her waist and bellowed. "Selmaa, Selmaa, come on, wake up pleeeaase." Usually, Selma would react to her cries. This time, although she heard her, she neither scolded nor stirred. She knew Görkem was trying to wake her up because she was hungry, but she didn't want to give in to her conscience. Clearly, they could feed themselves; all their griping was nothing but brazen laziness. In fact, the expression on Görkem's face gave away her secret: that she was strong enough for anything! She could feed herself perfectly well and meet all her own needs. Perhaps Selma couldn't bring herself to fully accept that a child might be no different from an uncaring, lazy, bloodsucking leech; whatever the case, she refused to acquiesce. She wasn't going to allow seemingly helpless creatures to disturb her peace, to take advantage of her.

She wasn't obligated to do anything. She kept her eyes closed and pulled the covers over her head. Görkem's yowling gradually faded, and finally, Selma managed to fall back to sleep.

Görkem, wary of calling out to Selma further, had quietly curled into a corner and was watching her mother's face. Softened by sleep, it was luminous.

She recalled the fights with Metin. Once, Selma had told Metin, "Don't let them poke their noses in things that are none of their business." She didn't recall who Selma had been talking about, but she remembered clearly that Metin was incensed. He had hurled the breakfast dishes in front of him. One of the glasses had shot up to the ceiling then hit the ground without breaking.

Selma had left home without touching anything, and had only come back after night had settled in. She had her hair bundled up, her ears were red, her hands blue. The children had tried to warm her up, hugging her and crying. Selma wasn't one for sentimentality. She had quickly grown weary of this superfluous display and made the children sit down on the sofa. She'd given them apples and oranges and let them get away with playing dangerous games with the fruit knives.

As Görkem remembered all this, she grew angrier. She wanted to grab a knife and cut Selma into pieces as she lay there under the covers; she inhaled the smell of blood, imagining the bedding heavy with it. Wasn't there a hole in this house where she could both hide and watch Selma?

Sometime later, Selma woke from her slumber, despite Görkem's silence. Slowly, she rolled her head left and right. When she saw Görkem hovering over her, she gazed at her daughter's face as if she were looking at the face of a complete stranger.

"I'm hungry, Selma. The baby is hungry, and Murat is hungry, too."

At that moment, what she felt for her daughter were the same feelings she would have for a stranger passing by at a distance. She shouldn't be faulted for not caring about feeding them. Why couldn't human offsprings fend for themselves a few months after being born, just like animals? If they couldn't develop the skills to feed themselves, they might as well die. What were these creatures, useless even to themselves, other than a burden on nature? These thoughts assailed her brain like a meteor shower. She shushed Görkem by bringing her finger to her lips. Görkem, powerless, began to weep.

The arteries of custom began to pump blood into Selma's body, and she got out of bed, instead of tending to the strange tree that had sprouted inside her. She went into the frosty kitchen and put two large potatoes in a pot. She took the baby from Murat, who was carrying it clumsily, and began to nurse it.

"Görkem, bring in some firewood."

The coal shed was at a distance from the house, on the other side of the school building that faced the village. It always stank of urine and feces because it was right next to the school toilets. Görkem was the one who most despised going there. She looked pleadingly at her mother's face, but she could tell that Selma had already made up her mind. She couldn't believe that she was sending her out to the coal shed in the terrible storm.

She put on her coat, which she had long outgrown. She wrapped her scarf around her neck, threw her boots on. She opened the front door, pushing with all her strength. Luckily, the storm had eased.

By the time she got to the shed she felt exhausted, as if she had been walking for days. Her hands were red from the cold, her fingertips numb. The cold permeated her body, stinging her skin. She managed to wrap her arms around two large chunks of wood. Mustering all her endurance, she started toward the house. As she hurried back, the frigid air flooded her lungs. Instead of invigorating her, the cold battered her; the burbling of the winter creek made her feel even colder. By the time she reached the school door on the other end of the building, she had no strength left. With a final push, she trudged on. She would rather carry out all of Selma's orders than put up with her angry, distrustful face. At last, she could see the door of the lojman. The storm had let up. All she heard now was the howling in the distant hills. After the calm, she knew, an even bigger storm would arrive, and it would snow even more. Görkem hated snow. She was sick of winter and the way it made everyone believe it would never end. In the winter months, she had to listen to Selma and Metin's fights, and their lovemaking.

She didn't understand Metin's interest in Selma. How could he love that woman? She was crazy. Out of the blue, you could find her excited, happy, all dressed up, her face painted, baking cakes and pastries or singing and dancing in the middle of the living room. At other times, she would be miserable, hateful, weepy, yelling and screaming suddenly as if the world was falling apart around her. And always she had a book with her; that's when she cut her ties with the world, withdrew into herself, noticed no one. Plus, she was ugly. She stared at you as if possessed, and the dark purple circles under her eyes aroused nothing but fear. With her protruding cheekbones, the suggestive curves of her lips, and her gap teeth, she was hideous. But for a reason she couldn't understand, Metin loved her. His gaze softened as if fearful of harming a fresh blossom, it wandered over her shapeless form, creating a warm, electric shield. Nothing in the world wounded Görkem as much as this attention. She found it unbearable that she never received even a fraction of Metin's affectionate gaze, that his pleasant, loving caresses, when directed toward his daughter, were overshadowed by hesitation, that it was Selma and not her who deserved his flattery. Their vulgar, excessive, disgraceful lovemaking cast black clouds over her eyes; her nose wished to inhale nothing but the smell of blood; she quivered with shame. Hatred invading her cells, a cyanide-laced knot traveled down her gullet into her stomach, poisoning her; her hands tingled with the desire to end the lives of both of them.

SELMA OPENED THE DOOR, AND GÖRKEM SAW THAT she must have just finished nursing the baby, since her shirt was buttoned haphazardly. The baby, disturbed by Görkem's noisy entrance, was awakened. Murat hurried to coax it back to sleep, knowing that neither Selma nor his sister would do anything about that. They had set everything else aside, hanging onto the one thing that mattered to them: War.

Görkem crouched by the door with the wood, pleading for help with plaintive eyes, but Selma's stern gaze ordered her to go to the living room instantly. Selma had been tiptoeing on the edge of insanity these past few days; what gave her away was not just her unsteady eyes, but her matted hair, her chalk-white face, and the way she was dressed, throwing on whatever she got her hands on. She walked around the house looking ridiculous. Lately, she had become more uncaring than ever. She didn't feed them, she didn't put them to sleep, she neglected their baths and routine care. Books, hours and hours of reading, outlandish thoughts distanced Selma from her responsibilities; in her own mind, she was rejecting motherhood. Stupid Selma! Stupid idiot! If you weren't going to love us, why did you make us?

Condemned to obey her mother's orders, she walked into the living room. When she saw the empty plates and the sliced bread on the table, she wanted to scream for joy. It turned out Selma had managed to cook for them after all.

Soon she was standing before her children with hot tarhana soup and potato salad prepared with tomato paste. Görkem and Murat began eating the food on their plates, while Selma stared absently at the table, not taking a single bite. She had no appetite.

They put wood, coal, and newspaper in the stove to light it again, and the house quickly warmed up. Thanks to Murat, the baby was in a deep, peaceful slumber. Everything seemed normal. They were full, warm, and, compared to a few hours ago, they felt at peace. All three were thinking of Metin, but since no one was too anxious, they did not brood on it for long.

They were accustomed to Metin's vanishing acts. As if he consorted from time to time with the jinn in supernatural fables and returned. And maybe he had a jinn wife, and mixed jinn-human children. As she stared blankly at the living room, Selma understood that what filled her head with these strange ideas was her peasant childhood, to which she was forever tethered. In the end, she smiled widely and gathered herself. During this brief daydream, Görkem had already scarfed down her food and was now making noise by tapping her plate with the spoon. Murat didn't finish his plate. The baby had managed to stay asleep in the armchair, despite the tense atmosphere of the house.

METIN HAD BEEN GONE FOR OVER TWO WEEKS.
Because the snow had blocked the roads, neither could he send
word nor did anyone arrive who could bring news. This had happened many times before. Once, he was gone for four days, once
for a week, once for three days, and another time, for five days.
He really was an odd man. Besides his disappearances, he had
also made a habit of building a soccer field in every village he was
assigned to. As soon as he set foot in a new village, he would start
surveying for a field suitable for playing ball, and he would always
find one. Next, he organized weekly tournaments. Selma attended
these festive events and enjoyed watching the games. Still, it was
pointless for her to struggle to act like a typical woman. She hadn't
warmed up to either married life or motherhood.

Selma treated her children honestly, true to her feelings. She
could do no more than that, though more was expected of her.
She saw love and affection as fabrications, words and emotions
that bound humans into a dark ignorance with dreadful chains.

Sometimes, she wished Metin wouldn't return. What she
wanted was to live forever in this mountain village, amidst
the snow, with that melancholy gloom. She didn't believe that

everything would change one day, that it would all work out. She didn't care much for people of faith, for those with hopeful dreams, and she certainly could not stand the zealots.

She realized she was being watched by her children. They had noticed that she was talking to herself and making odd facial gestures. Their anxious looks made her uncomfortable. She turned to face the wall and fixed her gaze on its blank surface, until she was distracted by Murat's voice. She answered "Yes?" in a soft voice, clearly less annoyed than by hearing Görkem, who sat beside him like a gooey puddle of fresh cement. They remained silent for a while.

Selma, pleased to be overcome by silence, just listened. She looked absentminded, withdrawn.

She reached for her tobacco case. Loosening the moist tobacco, she rolled it in paper. Something was bothering her. She wanted to disturb the silence.

"Murat! What day is it?"

And why did she ask this question? She didn't know.

Without hesitation, Murat said "Thursday." She cocked an ear to the outside; another storm was approaching.

GÖRKEM AND MURAT WERE PLAYING A STRANGE GAME
on the faded rug that covered the living room floor. They were
naming things they hated, and if they inadvertently repeated
something, they slapped each other as punishment. Selma
couldn't help eavesdropping on their game. She played with the
candle on the table, stabbing at it with a pin while experiencing
the astonishment of finding out a thing or two about her children's feelings for the first time.

"I hate the way Nuniş keeps disappearing all the time," said
Görkem. Nuniş was her doll, one of whose arms she had torn
off. A while back, when they were visiting one of Metin's teacher
friends, she had spotted Nuniş in the toy basket of this other
teacher's daughter, and had stealthily snuck it into Selma's hand-
bag. When they got home she had relished ripping off one of its
arms and named it "Nuniş," a slight variation on the name of its
previous owner.

Two days ago, Nuniş had disappeared again. She couldn't
help but suspect that the doll had a mind of its own, its own
secret world, and did as it pleased. In Görkem's mind, Nuniş was
a clever jinn that acted like a toy around humans. Whenever she

felt like it, Nuniş vanished into thin air. Ever since she brought the doll home, this vanishing act had occurred so many times that she couldn't play with it whenever she wanted. If she couldn't even control a toy, of course she would have to submit to Selma instead of bossing her around as she would like to do. And maybe it was Selma who kept hiding Nuniş. She wouldn't put anything past her. It irked her to consider this possibility. Frustrated, she repeated her sentence.

"I hate the way Nuniş keeps disappearing all the time!"

Right away, Murat followed suit, "I hate the way my truck has no wheels!"

Gathering all her strength, Görkem released her voice. "I hate eating apples!"

When Murat said, "I also hate eating apples," Görkem slapped him hard across the face with her small, powerful right hand. "No repeating!" she shouted.

His chubby cheek burning, Murat was startled, unsure how to react after this unexpected slap. His eyes filled with tears, but he braced himself not to cry, and went on with the game.

Everything that the two siblings hated stretched into a long list.

"I hate crying."

"I hate having to pee."

"I hate giraffes."

"I hate cheese."

"I hate watching movies."

"I hate painting rocks."

"I hate getting a tummy ache."

"I hate the computer."

"I hate my mother."

"I hate Selma, too."

Now, it was Murat's turn to slap. He got excited. His hands tingled. He sprang forward and slapped her hard. A rosy streak settled on Görkem's sallow cheek. Her face tensed with anger; her saliva, tainted with blood, oozed through her lips pursed with rage, trickling down her chin. She glared at Murat, stunned by the realization that she couldn't retaliate. This was the rule of the game. All she could do was bide her time until it was her turn, but the entire world, her jealous heart, her defiant, fiery personality, everything was goading her. She bit into her cheeks from spite. Swallowing the blood that welled in her mouth, she dug her nails into Murat's pink, unblemished cheek, scratching all the way to his neck. Still raging, she lunged on her brother like an arthropod leaping on its prey. She punched him, clawed at him over and over. It was as if the person beneath her, the one she was trying to rip apart, was Selma. Scratching, pinching, slapping, she tried to destroy the face that wouldn't go away, that wouldn't cease to exist, and she couldn't stop herself.

Selma had never heard so clearly that her children hated her. Although she knew that they weren't exactly on good terms, or that the children felt suffocated, she found it strange to hear that she wasn't loved at all. Her breathing became labored, and turning her face toward the wall, she pushed the pin she was holding into her finger. A sliver of blood spurted, flowed over the outline of her finger, and trickled onto the floor. As she watched the brief journey of the blood, she calmed down, remembering that she hated her children back. She was sickened by how they flaunted their innately malicious personalities, feeling no need to disguise them. What else could explain their audacity to say that they hated her, without mincing words, when she was sitting right beside them?

She thought of her own childhood. Had she loved her mother? She didn't know. Their relationship had been built on apathy rather than love. Perhaps that was more terrifying. Her children's hatred was preferable to apathy.

Oddly, she had no feelings toward her mother. She had never thought about this fact, always refraining from facing it. Try as she did as a child, not even a sprig of love for her mother ever greened inside her heart. She would neither feel sad when something bad happened to her mother nor reciprocate her mother's joy when they received any good news. And yet, her mother was better than most mothers; she had always been responsible, cheerful, understanding toward Selma.

Even when she had children of her own, she failed to empathize with her mother. Was this her nature? She had never asked herself such questions before. She had somehow been content with herself, imagining that no one minded her solitary existence. Living in one lojman after another, having children seemed to have changed everything. They made her ask uncomfortable questions, they blocked her escape. She bit her lip, moved her gaze from the ceiling to her finger, and noticed that the blood had congealed. She picked up a napkin from the table, spat on it and wiped her finger clean. Leaning back in her seat, she closed her eyes.

Someone was banging on the door. She sprang up, thinking it was Metin. The cold door handle awakened her senses. Her heart tightened, her body was overcome with anticipation. But standing before her was Yasin, with his guileless, well-meaning, stupid stare. He was again worried about the flag. He mumbled something Selma couldn't quite make out.

"I didn't hear you, Yasin, can you repeat?" she said, raising her voice. Selma's irritation made Yasin's already shy nature recoil even more. He paused briefly, then spoke in his gravelly voice.

"Selma Hanım, the flag is wrapped around the pole, I saw it when I was walking by, and I wanted to fix it." Selma was perplexed, her irritation turning to anger. "If you want to fix it, fix it, why are you telling me about it? I thought something happened to Metin, you scared me." Yasin's face turned beet red with shame. His voice trembling, he said, "Don't you worry Selma Hanım, God willing, I'm going to go to the township at the first opportunity. The storm ought to die down tonight, the weather will be good for three or four days, and I'll come back with Metin, you'll see."

"You know best. But Metin might not have gone to the town. Maybe you shouldn't go all the way there for no reason."

She slowly closed the door on him. She went to the living room and took up her cell phone. No reception. She looked around. Her eyes lingered on the landline. The green telephone with the futuristic look took her from the house and beamed her to a different place. Touching the phone, she felt like she could breathe again. She dialed the number for the teachers' lodge at the township, but then she hung up immediately. She didn't want to lift a finger for Metin. She was still furious about the way he had reacted to such a tiny squabble. He was often unreasonable when they fought, acting like a child angry with his mother. She hated that Metin was always self-righteous, ending all their arguments by shouting, making wild gestures. When that happened, she became confused, never knew what to do, whether to shout back at him or just walk away. In those moments she imagined that her husband's personality had escaped his body like a fugitive, that his foolish behavior had turned him into someone completely different.

Even though she needed Metin more than anything else, she believed it was best for everyone that he stayed in whatever hole he was hiding for the time being. She was fine with not seeing him for a while longer. She didn't want the children either. She had already seen enough of them.

Everything that happened to her was because of Metin's infinite love of children. No matter how much she had been in love with Metin, Selma had never wanted to have a child with him or anyone else. With all her heart, she had rejected the gift of fertility that nature had offered her as if it were some sort of blessing.

Yasin trailed back into her thoughts again. Oh, how she despised him. If only they let him, he would fix all the flags in the world. She realized she couldn't imagine him without a flag pole; she burst into an involuntary laugh. His eagerness to please others, his odd predilection for flag poles made her laugh. Dimwit! A true imbecile! She was caught in a flood of laughter, shuddering. The landscape joined in her laughter as Mount Süphan rose into the northern sky along with its shadow. Her children, the furniture she could never get used to, the gray walls that stretched into eternity—it was as if all of them were tickling her. The laughter turned into a hysteria that swelled inside her and cascaded from her lips, ending in sobs.

SHE INSTALLED HERSELF BY THE WINDOW. SHE looked at the soccer field, noticing how it stretched out into the emptiness as if it were one of Metin's limbs. Everywhere he ended up, Metin made it resemble himself. Every place had taken on his signature characteristics: his calm, his self-possession, his unusual steadfastness.

Selma clenched her teeth, her cheeks tensed. She could feel herself moving away from Metin. Questions, suspicions, meaningless sentences swirled in her head. Their love, was it really over? Or was it her anger that made her think so? She scanned the living room, the walls, her children. They had taken her love from her. Disgusting worms, they had desiccated her sexuality, they had robbed her of her appetite for a bit of skin, casting handfuls of earth over everything she enjoyed. The gray walls, the children that one by one settled within those walls, all of life, all of it sickened her!

How helpless she felt. She was lonelier than she had ever been. She could find no pleasure in the beauty of Lake Van as it clung to the edge of the horizon, nor find even the smallest excuse to stay alive. The landscape beyond the window sparkled with brilliance. Looking for a momentary respite, she fixed her gaze on the azure lake. She wanted to fill her eyes with the breathtaking triangle of Mount Süphan, the lake, and the horizon, to absorb the scenery into her being, to eternally bind herself to that magnificent triangle, if need be. Unfortunately, no amount of beauty would satisfy her. Her mind kept finding its way back to the things that exhausted her. She sank into hopelessness.

"Shall we go for a walk, Selma?"

Görkem's unexpected voice tore Selma away from her thoughts. Görkem had been energetic for the last few hours. If she encouraged her a bit further, they might even enjoy some idle chatter. Selma nodded. They put on their coats and went out. They were immediately overcome by the exhilaration of being truly outdoors for the first time in days. The piercing scent of snow filled the air. The sunlight, though timid, dazzled them both. Görkem pointed her finger to the mountain and said, "If only we could climb that mountain." Selma looked at her daughter for a while, then said, "You need to eat more rice for that." Görkem hated rice. "What does that have to do with anything?" she frowned. "I want you to grow taller." Her own words startled her. Clearly, she had uttered them because of the dreadful conventions of motherhood that had long nested deep in her consciousness. She wasn't really worried much about her daughter's height, but somehow, the sentence had just escaped her lips.

Görkem, hopeful that she could prove her mother wrong, assumed a confident tone, and said, "The Chinese eat rice all day, but they're all short."

"Where did you come up with that?" asked Selma, surprised.

"You said yourself that they were short."

Selma placed her hand on her daughter's shoulder while keeping her gaze fixed on Mount Süphan. "You're mistaken. True, Chinese people are short but if they hadn't been eating rice, we wouldn't even be able to see them."

The weather turned harsher. The snow-covered roofs of the village were visible in the distance. They looked back at their lojman and, like two birds beating their wings in unison, they both thought about how much they hated it. Noticing her mother's downcast face, Görkem asked, "Shall we walk to the village, Selma?" Selma shrugged half-heartedly. She could stay right there forever, she could stand absolutely motionless inside eternity.

Her desire to disappear was overpowering, and she gazed into the distance, all the way beyond the hills that rose across the plains. Over there, the sun was more alive, bathing the sky in luxurious light.

As if winter was on this side where she stood, and spring was on the other.

She squeezed Görkem's arm. "Let's go back in the house," she said.

The footprints they left behind remained on the surface of the snow all through the night.

THE BABY HAD FALLEN ASLEEP. SELMA WAS CURLED UP in a chair, reading, Murat was telling a story to his toys in a made-up language, and Görkem's eyes were fixed on her mother, waiting for the moment she would put down her book. Since she knew the awful consequences if she were to force Selma off her throne, Görkem waited for her to relax and voluntarily let go of her book. How much longer would Murat keep at his ridiculous game? His secret language had devolved into something that even he couldn't understand. The gibberish words and sounds were unintelligible, but from the way Murat kept rubbing the toys against each other, she could easily guess that his invented vocabulary concentrated around a topic with sexual content, and this irritated her. She felt the urge to pinch him, or at the very least to knock his toys down, which might relieve her anger.

But, clearly she could do neither while Selma sat there, having morphed into a celestial monument before her eyes. The joy Selma derived from books was so intense that neither Görkem nor anyone else could interrupt. Tired of waiting, Görkem decided to dethrone her, no matter the consequence. She would do this with such cunning that Selma wouldn't even have time to get angry. At the same time, she would put an end to Murat's stupid game. Stealthily, she glanced at Selma and at Murat, and headed to the kitchen. She pulled open the silverware drawer quietly and chose a sharp knife. She set the loaf of bread that was wrapped in a cloth on the counter in front of her and cut a slice halfway. Wasting no time, she slashed a deep cut into her index finger. With blood spurting, a victorious scream burst from her throat.

Murat heard his sister's scream and hurried to the kitchen, but Selma didn't budge. When he saw Görkem leaning on the bloodied counter, crying, he grabbed hold of her hand to stop the bleeding. Görkem was crying, not because of the pain in her finger, but because Selma wouldn't come down from her gilded throne. She gnawed at her lips in spiteful dissatisfaction, chewing at the flesh around her nails.

Murat rushed to find something to press against her finger. He searched and searched, but finally he ran to Selma. Kneeling by her feet, he stared at her with desperate, pleading eyes. Selma, aware of what was happening, gestured toward the ottoman across from her. Murat spotted the small crumpled hand towel, grabbed it and rushed back to his sister.

In her stubborn rage, Görkem didn't even see the towel Murat held out to her. He had to call out, "Sister, sister," several times.

"I'm not talking to you, I'm mad," shouted Görkem.

"What for?"

"You slapped me at the game!"

"But you slapped me too!"

"You can't slap me, you stupid idiot!"

"You can't slap me either!"

"I can!"

"You scratched my face, look, you can still see it."

"Shut up. Go away, I don't want that, let go of my hand!"

"It's bleeding hard, sister. M-o-o-o-mmy! It's bleeding hard. M-o-o-o-mmy!"

"Let go of my hand, it's not bleeding at all. I'm not talking to you!"

Murat continued to insist on holding her hand, and finally Görkem broke down, bawling. The more she thought about Selma's indifference, the more she yowled. She pressed her nail into the gash in her finger to make it bleed more.

The spectacle of agony went on for a few more minutes. Görkem screamed until she was exhausted. When she realized nothing could raise Selma from her seat, her crying stopped, giving way to maudlin sobs. Each sob shook her tiny chest, causing tremors in her body and signaling the likelihood that her next battle against Selma would be the bloodiest. She would prove to her that she was an invincible warrior.

Murat pulled the bleeding finger toward him and pressed it to the towel. If he could, he would stand there without saying a word until everything—his sister, his mother, the storm outside—completely disappeared. The painful bellowing, the sobbing that turned into a nervous breakdown, the punishing battles between Selma and Görkem, had all exhausted him. His small body could no longer fight the fatigue; and holding his sister's hand in his, he fell asleep on one of the floor cushions.

THE LAST DAYS OF JANUARY. THE VILLAGE, POISED TO withstand another month of violent storms, was a dark, iron-colored cloud settled among the mountains and hills. The villagers carried cowpats and wood from barns to homes, baked bread in pit ovens, fed the animals, and visited each other from time to time. The footpaths, the water canals, the poplar trees surrounding the plains alongside the dirt road that led to the asphalt, all were covered in ice, the soil had frozen through, Lake Van was covered in a thick layer of fog.

In the vastness of that scene, the lojman seemed smaller and smaller, squeezed into a ball, like a grenade that could explode at any moment.

Yasin was watching the smoke that rose from the lojman's chimney against the background of pure white snow. The Erciş Plateau stretched out before him. His random thoughts idled around fleeting topics, and his mind, unable to focus on anything else, honed in on the teacher's house. He wanted to know what went on inside that concrete dwelling, what Selma did throughout the day, how she walked around in the living room, the kitchen, down the hallway, how she treated her children. Selma's instability seemed more pronounced to him since Metin's departure. The children had looked neglected when he saw them last. He didn't even want to ask how the newborn was doing. Once or twice he had thought of congratulating Selma, but had been discouraged by her stern look that suggested quite clearly that there was nothing worth congratulating.

After a long trek, he reached the lojman. His heart sank at the sight of the abandoned school building. The dire conditions of the winter and Metin's absence had subdued the boisterous schoolyard. His own children were stuck at home, unable to go to school or play outside. The storm surges, the bone-chilling cold had made it difficult for children to play outdoors. They had to stay healthy. He wouldn't be able to bring them to the doctor. The nearest township clinic was hours away. God forbid, they could die on the way there. He pursed his lips. What could he do but pray for the winter to end soon? A heartfelt sigh escaped his nostrils.

He saw that the flag had again wrapped itself around the pole. It barely moved. He felt nervous and had to fix it. Hurrying his steps, he thought this could be a good excuse to talk to Selma, and maybe to see the children.

Holding onto the icy pole, he tugged on the cord. Because the flag had frozen around the pole, freeing it wasn't as easy as he had hoped. Soon enough, Yasin, who infused everything he did with traces of his stubborn nature, fixed the flag and watched it flutter against the sky. Taking confident steps, he walked up to the front door, but by the time he had tapped on it twice, he felt uneasy again. Görkem with her red curly hair opened the door. She was wearing only an undershirt. Yasin took a step back and, averting his eyes from the half-naked girl, asked whether Selma was home. Indifferent, Görkem called out "Selmaaa." While waiting for her mother to arrive, she didn't neglect to smile at Yasin, succeeding in finally bringing a warm smile to his face. Just when the lines upon the uninvited guest's face had started to relax, Selma appeared behind her daughter. Startled, Yasin forgot about using the flag as an excuse and blurted, "Any news of our teacher?"

Selma thought she saw a hint of death in Yasin's face and flinched. Fixing him in an icy stare, she said, "No, he is not back yet." A prolonged silence followed.

Yasin was wary of this woman who didn't speak much, who was reserved not just toward him, but even toward her own children. Until now, Selma had been open only with Songül, his wife, but even that openness was tentative. Every so often, when Songül fired up the pit oven or when she headed to the mountainside to gather herbs, Selma would join her. Hours later, when Yasin asked "What did you two talk about?" a terse, repressed, mocking "Nothing" would escape Songül's lips. And it was true that they didn't talk about anything of substance. Selma was the type of stingy friend who shared little of her thoughts, emotions, or intentions.

Yasin never understood how Metin could tolerate her strange personality. He couldn't make sense of how she never cooked, how she left her children's care to her husband, how she idled about most of the time. Take, for instance, her bizarre attitude toward the superintendents who had come to check on the school. At the end of their visit, they had expected to rest awhile, but Selma had neither made tea for her guests nor even smiled at them. She just sat on the chair she had placed next to the front door, took regular drags on her hand-rolled cigarette, and kept muttering, her displeasure clearly written on her face.

The superintendents, feeling more than spurned, had initiated an investigation against Metin as soon as they left the village. In truth, her behavior had secretly delighted Yasin. What she did was a rebuttal to the officials' self-satisfied, condescending attitude. Selma had dismissed them the way she dismissed everyone.

Dismiss the shadows, if we want. What of it?
Denial is now useless.

SHE WAS POISED FOR A LONG JOURNEY, ONE WITH NO turning back. A dark, irresistible landscape awaited her. Once she took the first step, everything would change. A short stretch at first, then a little longer, and a little longer. . . . She had never felt she belonged to this place, and she would never return. She put on her coat, wrapped a scarf around her neck, and tied her boots. She could see no one in the direction of the snow-covered plains. She wanted to walk the icy road all the way to Erciş. With every step, she savored the poems in her mind, the looming presence of Mount Süphan. She recited to herself the small clusters of verse that came rolling in.

I saw you for the last time
Asleep, curled up in your crib, hurt . . .

She wandered aimlessly along the shore. The small, dark cavities of her footsteps in the snow advanced within the expanding silence. She should never return to her children, to the gray house, just vanish into the blue expanse of the lake.

Her hands clasped over her stomach, she listened to her surroundings, filling her ears with the wind, the indistinct voices of the villagers, the sounds of winter animals, leafless trees.

I have tasted so little of the world, she thought. She wanted to walk out upon the lake and disappear into the horizon, where her field of vision ended, somewhere over the plains. She was trapped in a melancholy so powerful that it was clear she could not remain on the shore much longer.

Completely worn out, she slipped her hands in her pockets and turned her back to the lake. The lojman loomed larger than before. She resented knowing that she would return to the grayness that beckoned her, that promised her safety. Against her will, she began running toward the house, unable to restrain her obstinate feet. Like a snail torn from its shell, she was bewildered when she couldn't feel the house over her body. She couldn't resist rejoining the gluey, mucous coilwork. The slime that enveloped her insisted on its demands. Total submission, blindness, enslavement . . . She was someone who repented every time but sinned again at the first instance of weakness. She pitied herself. She was a pathetic coward. As she reached the front door, nothing was visible except the smoke rising from the village chimneys and the endless icy blue. In that vast landscape, she was a scrap of newsprint on a collage. Not of that setting, yet part of it just the same.

Far from the village, the asphalt road leading to Erciş looked like a white, living reptile that stretched into nothingness. Her hands, her face were beet red. She hadn't realized how exhausted she was by the cold until she arrived at the door. In her eyes, on her face, there were no hints of discontent nor concern for her children. She had forgotten everything as she hurried toward the lojman. Once there, she rested her head gently against the outer wall, slowly coming back to reality. She closed her eyes, her ears perked up. She heard sobs that sounded almost like someone was choking. She didn't want to know or hear what was happening, or that the sobbing belonged to her baby who had been hungry for some time. She wanted to rest against the wall a little longer, to keep her eyes closed, to just breathe. A familiar sensation took hold of her, pulling her in. When she felt it reach even the whites of her eyes, she closed her mouth shut.

Now she could hear Görkem's and Murat's voices blending with the baby's crying. Her eyes burned. A few teardrops ran down her cheeks. Her chin trembled, she couldn't stop the pounding of her heart. The hot tears multiplied, trickling down her cheeks to her chin, then to her chest. She was floating upon a pool of tears like a drop of oil. She needed to believe that she hadn't gone mad, that she wasn't contriving excuses to evade motherhood. She was afraid, afraid of her children, of her baby who didn't even have a name, of the way it was always hungry. The voices grew louder. They leaked from the lojman's walls and wrapped around her throat, they seeped under her skin, into her blood. She was being poisoned, she was dying, her children were doing to her what winter did to the lake.

She had to put an end to the torture, she had to bash her head against the wall until she felt nothing.

Harder, more violently . . . She bowed her head, touched it with her fingers. A lump had formed on the side of her forehead within seconds. There was no blood, not even a scratch. Only a little lump had emerged; her anguish had turned into a comic protrusion on her head.

"SELMA, THERE WAS A MAN IN MY DREAM. HE SAID HIS name was Yusuf. He was inside a wooden trunk, folded in two. He looked at me and said something. Three times! I was so scared. Hold me, please!"

Selma was sound asleep when Görkem had her nightmare right around daybreak and rushed in to snuggle in her mother's arms. She could not erase the image of the emaciated man with his brittle skin, his elongated nose and bulging eyes. It was horrifying. She trembled like a leaf. He looked like a corpse, and it terrified her.

He was squeezed inside a tiny trunk. Every now and then, he poked out his head and said unintelligible things. Görkem, drenched in sweat, opened her eyes, nearly freezing. Although she knew it was all just a nighmare, its effect was unbearable and had made her run to her mother.

She shook her and shook her but Selma wouldn't wake up. Her sleep, always deep, was even more dense this time, impenetrable. Selma fell asleep as if she would never wake up again, as if that was exactly what she wanted.

Görkem kept poking at her mother until she was convinced that she would not wake up. Still caught in her nightmare, she crawled into bed next to Selma without her consent. Her body was warm. She curled toward Selma's belly and wrapped herself in one of her arms. She began to calm down. Even if the ghoul in her dream were to return, it could do nothing to her now.

Her sleep blended into her mother's dense sleep. Like drops of mercury that fuse together. Now she was walking in a pastel landscape, soaring with each step. Serene, worry-free.

WHEN SHE WOKE UP IN THE FIRST LIGHT OF THE morning, feeling more rested than usual, she was surprised to find Görkem curled up next to her with her tiny feet drawn to her belly. She pulled the covers over her, trying not to wake her up. In a few seconds, she heard the peaceful murmurs of her baby. It must have woken up right after her. When she turned her head toward the murmurs, she saw the baby at the foot of the bed.

Strangely, she could anticipate the baby's movements. She watched it with interest for a while, the same way she watched Görkem. Its sparse hair, long fingers, its toothless, endearing mouth that resembled an old man's. Its skin was much darker than Görkem's, more like Metin's.

When she picked the baby up to check the diaper, she realized how much she missed Metin. A quiet voice inside her told her that he was alright, that he would soon return.

She felt peaceful. With a sweet smile on her face, she changed the baby and nursed until it fell asleep. She observed the eyes motionless under the translucent eyelids, the feathery eyelashes that glistened in the morning light, the fresh, small indentations under the eyes, velvety like rosebuds.

Laying the baby next to Görkem, she went to the living room, muttering poetry. The verses triggered her affection for Metin once again. She smiled faintly, repeated the lines in her head.

The glorious awakening of the reckless soul, the forsaken youth
The line permeated her entire being, quickly and effortlessly, like a protective spell from subterranean spirits. Clouds spread across the sky, crowding out the face of Mount Süphan and mirroring the clouds in her soul. The mountain took on a metallic color as Selma walked past the gates of poetry. Cracks, crevices widened and offered her a dazzling glare that would never let her rest. She tried to grasp the thing that quivered in her soul. Reciting poetry meant scorching the flower of motherhood with a flamethrower. She leaned her face against the back of the armchair and curled up, lost in questions and thoughts. How was it that the dazzling variety of colors in nature could coexist in such harmony, why could they change, fade, and flare up again? Poetry, too, was like this. It moved along through each verse, shook you to the core with its self-contained beauty, aroused, wounded, and bled you, and yet, in the end, did not disrupt anything.

At nighttime
He looked for himself
As if looking
For a single insect among the grass
And called out from a distance
"Wait"

AT THIS TIME OF THE YEAR, SELMA FELT LIKE SHE WAS the only one who truly appreciated the mallards that arrived at the reedbeds of Lake Van, exhausted after their long flight from northern countries. As she stood by her window illuminated by the evening sun, she would gaze wistfully at the flocks in the distance, reflecting on pleasant memories. Observing nature and life from poetic angles helped to allay her physical exhaustion. She didn't think of poetry as good, bad, or extraordinary. For her, poetry was pure experience; neither good, nor bad, nor marvelous, it could not be exalted or corrupted. Its essence crystallized and then spread out to achieve its self-made form, digging through, mining the elements of sound and rhythm. The darkness of Mount Süphan and the darkness of Lake Van meet at a single line, the fiery redness of the evening settles over the village like a haze, and poetry achieves equilibrium in order to destroy it, not to preserve it. As she often did in those moments when she didn't feel like answering the questions that arose inside her, Selma kneaded her face with her hands, held her breath, tried to stop time. Who are you? Why aren't you anywhere else on this earth but here, in Erciş, in this village?

Selma never wanted to answer these questions. She insisted on not understanding her mistake, on locking horns instead. She wanted earthquakes, howls, screams to break through the questions swarming her brain. When she found no inner strength, she fantasized about someone killing her. She imagined a hand pushing her off the cliff, the eyes of someone plunging a knife into her belly. But, why couldn't she do it herself? Why couldn't she put an end to the pain that had been burning in her chest since the day she was born?

She wasn't a coward. Nor was she meek. She wasn't stupid. She possessed the strength, the will, the ability to end this wretched existence. Were her children the reason she didn't do it? Or was it her husband, whom she loved? Or poetry? No! Neither her children who resembled little worms nested inside a fresh fruit, nor her husband who made her body tremble with love, nor the poetry that added meaning to her life! Not one of these was strong enough to make her abandon her death wish. The only thing binding Selma to life was perhaps an authentic agony that she still longed for. She didn't want to leave this world before experiencing a pain immense enough to decimate her. The longing for a sharp pain that pierced her chest, a pain that she would feel down to the marrow of her bones, that would leave her breathless . . . that was the only reason she still lingered by the cliff.

GÖRKEM COULDN'T FALL ASLEEP. SHE FELT A strangeness in her belly, an agitation she couldn't describe. Maybe it was the alignment of the constellations in the sky that kept her awake, or the storm that made everything more unbearable than ever. She didn't know, all she knew was that if she didn't fall asleep right away she was going to suffocate from boredom. She noticed the baby. Its tiny body had astonished her from the beginning. What a strange creature it was with the folds of its clumsy arms, its small, flat head, its short neck. She tucked her index finger into the baby's limp fist that had fallen to the side. A warmth she had never experienced before spread from her finger to her entire body. She inhaled the sweet, warm smell emanating from the baby's neck, which eased the disquiet of her stomach. The light from the baby's eyes reached her, enfolding her with the secret kinship of siblings. She relished the intoxicating feeling, listened to the sounds of the secret bond between them. The tempest raging in her chest began to calm.

Yet, something odd kept flickering on the baby's face. It resembled Selma, she thought. In an instant, the peaceful halo the baby had created slipped through her fingers. She examined the baby at length, its hair, eyes, nose, mouth, chin. No, this was not a physical similarity, but something about the two of them being made of the same supernatural matter. The baby bore traces of the arrogance that defined Selma's intellect. Revolted, she pulled her finger from the baby's hand. Her eyes filled with tears of jealousy. She turned her back, facing the other side of the bed.

Selma had finally succeeded in leaving a piece of herself on earth. It meant that she would never cease to exist, become nothing, turn into an eternal silence. Cunningly, she was taking over the world. And doing so from within one single point-source. Selma had chosen not her but this earthworm to be the beneficiary of her physical inheritance, yet another example of her unfairness that swallowed the world whole. She hated her mother more than she ever had in her short little life. She wanted to tear the baby away from sleep, to blot out its face that bore the traces of Selma.

She clenched her teeth. The discomfort in her stomach grew, spreading all the way to her chest. No chance that she would fall asleep. She was angry with god for giving her a woman like Selma for a mother. She was never going to ask him for anything ever again. Not that he had really granted any of her wishes. Had he been been trustworthy, he wouldn't have sent a calamity like Selma upon them. When it was her turn to stand before god, she wasn't even going to look at his face.

Oh, Selma! Endless anguish. Festering wound. Poisonous green vomit! She must be extinguished, crushed, eliminated. Görkem had to find the way to destroy everything that belonged to her.

THE FIRST LIGHT OF DAY FLOWED FROM THE CLEAR blue sky and bathed Görkem's face. Her anger had kept her awake into the morning. Despite her exhaustion, she stared into the wall with spiteful, unblinking eyes while she listened to the song Selma was humming. If her stare were a laser beam, the wall would have disintegrated by now. What a dreadful voice, she thought to herself. Dreadful like the self-assured, raspy voices of old grannies. She promised herself that she'd tell her mother this when the time was right. Selma wouldn't like being compared to an old granny one bit.

She sat up in bed, pressed her nose against the cold window to ease her discomfort, if only a little. She watched the bare poplar trees in the distance enduring the winter, the people in the village who hurried from their homes only to hurry back. She gazed at the flagpole rising from the schoolground, at the billowing flag. Everything was losing color, vitality, as time passed. The world was quickly growing old. She took a deep breath, feeling the endless doldrums inside her, realizing that there was no trace left of her childhood. A happy childhood? It had never knocked at her door. She wanted nothing that belonged to childhood, and wished she could grow up at once. She tried to mimic one of Selma's grown-up gestures to prop up her body, but couldn't perform the stupid movement. Maybe her hands would not be the first things to transition to maturity. Instead she tried that know-it-all, detached, loftier-than-god expression she was used to seeing on Selma's face. She gave her eyes the blank stare of a dead fish. For her, Selma was nothing but a fish long dead. The only fish that, owing to its gloominess, had ever managed to drown in the sea.

When Görkem entered the living room, Selma was humming a ridiculous pop song, not the same tune she'd heard a minute ago. Görkem watched the stupid expression pasted on her face for a while. Selma had ensconced herself on her fancy throne, as always. One raised eyebrow, pure attention, she was reading a book she had picked from her horrible bookshelf, her most priceless possession, which she could ignore only for a few hours at a time, at most. Görkem remembered once again that all her life, Selma had never looked at her with that same interest or care.

If it hadn't been for Murat tugging on her sweater and inviting her to play with the broken toys he'd scattered over the carpet, Görkem could have cracked in two from spite. Luckily, her brother, clueless about everything, had yanked her out of these agonizing thoughts. Poor Murat, she thought, as she accepted his invitation to play, he doesn't even know what a fearsome demon Selma is.

Murat's submissive nature irked her; she decided to tell her brother everything, and come up with a scheme to destroy Selma. She was going to tell her brother that Selma didn't care about her children at all, that she was a selfish woman who cared only about her books and those poems she read so ecstatically, that she didn't think of Metin, not even once, since he'd left, that she gave birth to a baby just like herself and didn't even bother to feed it. It was about time for the demon she kept hidden in secret nooks around the house to show itself. With the perfect plan, they could get rid of her at once and forever. Görkem was ready to take full responsibility. She wasn't afraid of anything; the idea of destroying Selma comforted her, made her happy.

Lost in her whirlpool of thought, she didn't even notice that Selma had gone out to the coal shed. She continued to play with her brother until she heard a distant, muffled shout. She listened. When the shouting wouldn't stop, she realized the voice belonged to her mother. She stopped playing and dashed outside. Once by the coal shed, she realized that, somehow, the door had closed and Selma was trapped inside. She was about to open the door, but she stopped. For a moment, the clouds in her head cleared and her mind lit up like a red kite in a clear blue sky. Once she knew that she wasn't going to lift a finger to free Selma, her foul mood lifted easily.

Selma punched the wall, shouted, tugged on the door handle, trying to find a way to open it. Overhearing her desperation delighted Görkem. She wanted to hear her plead more, beg for help, she yearned to hear her scream desperately.

Excited by the sounds that filled her ears, she relished the joy she felt. She didn't even feel cold in the frigid weather. She was ecstatic, lost in the music of her mother's horrible pleas; she could rescue Selma in a second if she pleased.

Exhausted from shouting now, Selma waited silently in the coal shed, sensing that someone was on the other side of the door. At first, she thought it was Yasin and asked him for help. Getting no response, she realized it was someone else, who had been out there for some time. She pressed her ear, her cheek, her hands against the door and tried to sense who it was that didn't want to help her. Like insects that identify their enemies with their antennae, before long, she knew. It was Görkem.

WHEN SELMA WALKED INTO THE LIVING ROOM, SHE saw her children sitting among scattered objects. She was brimming with the desire to destroy everything in her path, conscience be damned. The village, the school, the house, her children, Metin, all of them were stuck in her throat, choking her. Then she decided, suddenly, that she wasn't going to remember the horrifying moments in the coal shed. She was going to forgive her daughter's betrayal, erase from her memory that Görkem had heard her but hadn't come to her aid. She would swallow her resentments, try to live on, seemingly resigned to her fate, live as someone else, keep on breathing in her false, foul existence, pretending to be alive. That clammy, suffocating feeling overcame her movements, her body, and finally, her entire being. Her words, quietly mumbled at first, soon became frenzied, meaningless sentences that issued from her lips as she trembled in a delirious rapture.

"There's life outside—thunder, rumble, landslide—sounds exist to tell human beings that we don't really exist—we don't— Metin and I don't exist—this mountain village, this lojman, they don't exist—Murat and the baby don't exist—grayness, snowstorms, long roads, death don't—sinkholes do—black holes, space exist but not Görkem—not poetry, not the howls—the holes between our thighs, wet, curvy holes, they exist—vile whirlpools, yes, but not us—no hope, no crying, no daydreams—none of our fears—not our infernal geography

"our eyes that detect light, our souls, they exist

"something flows from our abdomen, our bodies, and mixes with life, something colorful, bright, liquid, something that can sneak into any place—there is no gossip that makes our ears ring, only endless murmurs—no sand dunes formed by windstorms, no desert flowers, nor chess—toilets exist, piss, insects, rodents, borers, gnawers, stingers exist, so does mercury—my heart doesn't exist; my throat does—physics, no, allegory, yes, rhythm, no, beats, yes—there are pills, there is a satanic battle—there are frame-ups, weapons, exploding floors, weddings, and electric saz—we don't exist, forbearance exists, graveyards, too—no pages, no holy mosques, no wellsprings—there's cyberpunk, pornpolitics, hajj—no hot springs, no volcanic or tectonic rocks—no obstructions, no painful serums, methane gas or citric acid—there's vapor, there's sulphur—apricot crates, slit cheeks, cold climates, the Night of the Ascension, and the torso—there's habit, attachment, there's bonding—and suckling—there's fibula, no tibia, no scapula!—there are figs dipped in flour, plants whose sap causes lesions, itchy skin, fragrant handkerchiefs, profanity, there is forgetting . . ."

Her mind was out of control, spinning and swerving in the world of objects. There is, there isn't, there is, there isn't, there is, there isn't . . .

"no courtesy, no gaudy scarves, no white heels, no mucus—no head buried in the sand, no rats lost in mazes, no smallpox, or malaria—no supplies, dark nights, hypocrisy, expropriation, expansive landscapes—there's no Metin—no township, no tree-toads, no lake shore, monsters, wild weeds, no red rope, no dull days, no passion—there is the stratosphere and the ionosphere, there's decadence, there is swimming, there's getting somewhere, there's perfect form—no syncopation, no vibration, there's only sound—no mechanism for movable structures—there are active apposable organs—no deltoid, no bucal corridor, no diabetes—no sanctions—there's serratus anterior, there are oblique muscles—my tears exist, borders exist, there are letters, there is abstract art—excitement exists, my hands don't . . ."

Her eyes stern, bulging, she could not stop her mind from spewing out increasingly meaningless sentences. She was hearing a voice rising from her abdomen to her ears, first faint, then sharp, strong, staggering. The voice reverberated "Görkem! Görkem! Görkem!"

"no description, no suspension, no pickle juice, bitter iron, no roots—there's submission, enzymes, theoretical mathematics "no pile of bread, no border guards . . ."

She watched, amazed, her children sending their gnarled roots into the ground. Görkem, spreading over her body like poison ivy, was a grotesque betrayal, a horrible disease made of her own flesh and blood, bent on consuming her. She despised her daughter enough to slash her pubescent curves. Crush her joints, carve holes into her heels, stab her hands with nails, brand her eyes with hot skewers, injure her soul irreparably. She ought to trample her life starting to sprout like a delicate sapling, destroy her dark personality before it could mature any further. She would plunge her head in the waters of Lake Van and dig her a grave in the snow. As she watched her slowly freeze, she would make sure that she saw the expression of joy on her face.

"there are no poison frogs, no roasted potatoes, no femur, no harmful last will and testament, no law—there are cats, no birds, no giraffes, no breeze, there's halvah—there's the pious community, there are organisms, there's no cancerous skin—there are domesticated flowers—no grumbling, no gossip—there's amputation, deepthroat, discipline, there is a bucket—rhythmic gait, long distance run, catnip, beatings, the sales and marketing of enema equipment, but not you—there are ulcers, hemorrhoids, ankylosing spondylitis, muscles, joints, the brain, there is grasping, drifting—no corrosion, no tendinitis, there are electric outlets, there's dilation—there's planking, rigidity, thinning, corrosion, and beams, pulleys, sheer strakes, transom seats—there's a scorpion in the zodiac—there are swivels, no hooks—he is not, we are—I'm not, they are!"

GÖRKEM, DELIGHTING IN HER MOTHER'S PENANCE, continued to play on the floor. While she kept an eye on Selma's bizarre, wildly unhinged behavior, she also tried to keep Murat under check. Watching Selma's defeat, she waited with hopeful anticipation for her rotting, weary existence to disappear. It was enchanting. She couldn't keep from watching everything she did, she was drawn to her like a magnet. Stupid Selma! Idiot! Die already.

She could see into the weakest regions of Selma's soul. She was privy to all the actions she had ever performed or would perform, from the way she picked up her books to the way she curled up in a corner, lost in daydreaming. She had won. Despite her cries for help, she had stood at the door to the coal shed, not lifting a finger; then, she had just walked away. The game was hers. Selma's defeat and her helplessness were her rewards. The false displays of independence she had learned from books had proved useless. And so, she had fallen off the pedestal that had never belonged to her. Real life had shown her otherwise.

She had finally scared Metin away with her nonsense. How she used to throw whatever she could grab at poor Metin. Vile mother, the most appalling of all humans. She had been jealous of Metin's affection for his children. And if Metin was never coming back, Görkem would derive the greatest joy from watching the cloud of remorse on her face.

THE STUBBORN LANDSCAPE AROUND LAKE VAN offered hope to the straggler greenheads and mottled mallards left behind from the migration. Snow cascaded down the nearby hills to join the waters of the lake; as the slow rumble spread over the plains, cormorants, common ravens, magpies, blue tits, nuthatches, long-tailed tits were absorbed in a careful search and inspection.

As the first light of day descended onto the plains, one of the mallards resting in the hot springs fell prey to its own inexperience. The ice surrounding the reedbeds expanded and gaped. The mallard, shaking itself methodically from head to tail, was about to take flight when its webbed feet got caught in the ice at the edge of the spring. The hapless creature was immediately trapped. Beating its wings, the duck struggled to free its feet, but it was too late. The flock had long disappeared from the Erciş Plateau, and the mallard was paying for its carelessness. It made weeping sounds, then took to harrowing calls. But nothing came of its flailing or cries. It stared at the horizon that stretched all the way to Çaldıran, blinking. As if resigned to its fate, it tucked its bill inside its breast feathers.

Among the reeds, the neon-green head glowed like an emerald in the sunlight reflecting off its feathers. The mallard heard footsteps fast approaching and it shuddered, thrashing about in panic. As the footsteps came closer its terror multiplied. It tried spreading its wings, but to no avail. Now it felt a hand upon its head. The hand caressed its feathers, softly closed around its body. Soon, the mallard was overcome with warmth. It calmed down, relaxed, and was filled with trust.

That warm hand belonged to Görkem, who had sought to escape the suffocating air of the house.

She had left the lojman at daybreak, played in the snow for a while, and walked all the way to the lake to pass the time. Wandering among the reedbeds, she had been excited to see the mallard and decided right then to take it home with her.

With an uncontrollable burst of love, she longed to grab the mallard and hold it. She could take home this beautiful, lonely creature, and mother it. That way, Selma could see what true motherhood was like. She was going to love the mallard with all her heart and dedicate all her time to this bird. She gazed into the mallard's eyes and smiled. She couldn't contain her excitement, her heart beat rapidly, her hands trembled.

Quickly, she grabbed the mallard with both hands. Trying to lift its body, gripping it from both sides, she realized that the animal was stuck in the ice. She started tugging. She pulled with such determination that, finally, the mallard's feet remained lodged in the ice and she had its body in her arms. The mallard, drenched in blood, wailed in anguish.

Görkem was stunned. She stood among the reeds, covered in the mallard's blood. When it seeped through her sweater and she could feel it on her belly, she came to her senses. Holding it up, she examined the mallard's wings and the hollows where the legs had been, thinking that the creature might still be alright. Her excitement had given way to distress, but then she thought, if it's making noise, it's still alive, and she could think of nothing other than asking for Selma's help. She set out toward the house, weeping more mournfully than the mallard.

Selma tore herself from her slumber and ran to the door. She was frightened. Long overcome by her conviction that some bad news from Metin would sooner or later arrive to rattle her, she inevitably took every signal of alarm as a bad omen. When she opened the door, she found Görkem standing before her. She was about to ask her what on earth she was doing outdoors in the cold of of daybreak when she noticed the mallard she was holding tightly in her arms.

"I tore off its feet. Selma, don't let it die, please!"

Keeping her calm, Selma took the wounded creature from Görkem's tense arms. After carefully inspecting its body and the holes where its feet would have been, she placed it back in Görkem's arms.

"It's going to die. It won't make it. Let's bandage the wounds anyway."

A wave of pain spread across Görkem's face. Were it not for the lively red curls obscuring her features, Selma would have noticed this wave of pain, so profoundly felt. Görkem couldn't believe how casually she had declared, "It's going to die." A dagger to her heart would have likely caused her less pain.

They brought the duck to the living room. Görkem placed her new guest near the wood stove in the middle of the room so it could warm up. Selma began treating the beautiful creature whose body gave off wet-smelling vapors. The wounded mallard buried its bill into its feathers, trying to endure the pain as best it could. The poor thing blinked, bracing for the inevitable moment of battle. Selma, in awe of this formidable creature, so strong despite its anguish, caressed the mallard's head while attending to the wounds. The unexpected care her mother showed the mallard stung Görkem's hurt and frightened heart.

Judging from the brilliant colors and the dainty body, their guest had to be a female, they thought. Selma refrained from asking any questions. She remembered the day she had noticed Görkem's temperament when she tore off one of Nuniş's arms.

Devastated, Görkem watched Selma, and the tenderness that accompanied her superhuman effort to help the mallard. How come this monstrous woman could show the mallard a care she never showed her children?

Indeed, Selma found it more tolerable to rush to the aid of the mallard than to feed and look after her children. With quick steps, she hurried to the medicine cabinet in the kitchen. Back with some cotton, hydrogen peroxide, iodine tincture, and gauze, she told Görkem to hold the duck between her legs. She started cleaning the holes left from the torn legs. After examining the animal's wounds, she bandaged the bloody area.

The mallard let its body go limp. Nestled in the designated spot beside the wood stove, it buried its head in its breast. This time, the duck kept its eyes closed for a long time. Selma turned to her daughter, who waited for some explanation, and told her that perhaps their guest would make it.

THE MALLARD OPENED HIS EYES, AND PULLING HIS bill from his downy breast, must have gaped at this strange, completely unfamiliar place. A terrifying place, one he could neither grasp nor recognize. There was no sky, nor the majestic rise of Mount Süphan, nor the azure of Lake Van. Fluffing his feathers, tucking each back in place, perhaps he tried to recollect how he ended up here. Were it not for his internal clock, he would not even have known it was morning. As far as he could tell, there was no sky above this hell. Who had put him inside this gray box? His heart beat so quickly, he was afraid of dying. Quietly, he craned his head, looking for a way out into the sky. There was none. Feeling what must have been an excruciating pain below his abdomen, thoroughly exhausted, he realized he had no choice but to wait. He tried to prop up his body, made an effort to crawl, which only intensified the pain. He moved his wings. The pain, now unbearable, reminded him that a human had torn off his legs and brought him to this place. He was seized with fear. So, this was what human nests looked like. Colorless, cramped, terrifying . . . Small boxes purposefully built to deprive themselves of sunlight. The ground had no soil, but instead a strange substance that aroused eerie sensations. All of this must have been utterly baffling. What creature capable of feeling the wind against its skin would choose to squeeze itself into such a place? He had never imagined humans to be such fools.

"LOOK, SHE'S STILL THERE, IN THE SAME SPOT!"
Görkem shrieked with joy.

"No, not the same; it looks like she moved a little," Murat said.

"No, no!" insisted Görkem. "She's right where I left her yesterday, see?"

This time there were notes of anger added to her piercing cries. Murat eagerly leapt forward, full of confidence, and pointed with his finger to the spot where the duck's tail rested.

"Yesterday, when you put her next to the stove, her tail touched the red stripe on the rug; see, now it's on the blue." He extended his right hand, and aligning his thumb with the tail, he came up with his own calculation, "Ooo, she's two hands farther than before!" he cried excitedly.

Sensing defeat, Görkem was enraged.

"That's my duck, get it? I found her!"

The disagreement was building up to a small-scale battle. Selma strained to lift her head, heavy as a rock, and thought again how she couldn't endure her children's voices for much longer, how much she wished they would disappear for good. Görkem's voice especially drove her crazy. She rose from bed and made her appearance at the living room door with a cold, cheerless face. Her children didn't need to see that she was at the door; they had already sensed her and stopped bickering. They moved away from the mallard. Selma, wrapped in a blanket of imperviousness, assumed a bizarre trot and went over to the animal to inspect. She noticed that the mallard looked much better than it had yesterday. When she kneeled for a close-up look, Görkem and Murat huddled around her. The three of them encircled the animal. As Görkem poured her angry, insecure energy all over her, Selma calmly lifted the mallard's body and examined the wounds. They seemed quite good. She quickly declared her prognosis so she wouldn't have to hear Görkem, who appeared ready to pose a question.

"She'll make it."

Görkem was uneasy that Selma didn't even give her an opportunity to mother the bird herself. She declared the mallard off limits, casting warning glances at whoever came too close. She had done it again. She had taken her duck from her!

She wanted to ask Selma many questions but bit her lips, knowing that none would be answered.

"When is Metin coming back?" she finally asked.

"In a few days," said Selma. Görkem was surprised how, at the mention of Metin, Selma's voice always softened, took on a pastel color.

Metin's name was like a painkiller that relaxed Selma. She missed him very much. If only she knew that he was fine. She didn't deserve to be punished like this. To escape the chaos in her mind, she turned to her children and asked, "Are you hungry?" In truth, she didn't want to feed them or even see them.

"Yes!" cried Murat excitedly. "Let's fry some potatoes, mommy."

SOMETIME IN THE EVENING, THEY HEARD NOISES outside. Selma anxiously rushed out the door. Yasin had grabbed hold of a huge snow shovel, and was clearing the front yard of the school. When he noticed Selma looking at him, he felt the need to explain himself.

"Selma Hanım, I'm clearing the schoolyard to make it easy for the children. Once I'm done here, I'll shovel the front of the house."

Selma didn't react. Yasin felt obligated to say something to break the silence. "Is our teacher back yet?"

Selma gestured "no" with her head and went inside; she didn't care to speak with Yasin any more.

She was sick of Yasin showing up every chance he got, reminding her about the work that needed to be done around the school. Raising the flag, tidying the flowerbeds around the building, painting the classroom walls; and the way he started his every sentence with "Selma Hanım," his endless questions and minutiae were insufferable. Now he had made Metin his business, too, standing by the door, asking in his hideous voice,

"Selma Hanım, is there any news of our teacher?" And, oh, his well-meaning, childlike eyes, so sickening.

Selma couldn't understand why Yasin was so insistent, so anxious and concerned about details that, to her, were stupid and inconsequential. At times, when she sat on the rocks at the edge of the dirt field and stared at the school building, so solid and impervious, doubts crept into her mind. What could possibly be the reason Yasin did all this? This school and the lojman, sitting like cow splatter right in the center of a peerless scene, ought to have been more overbearing for him than she could even imagine.

She went over to the window and watched Yasin. His kyphotic spine disappeared and reappeared among the snow mounds. He was a stain upon the snow, a mechanical limb that extended from the school building. Lately, Selma had been thinking that everything she saw around her was an extension of the school and the lojman.

When she heard the baby's voice, she shed her daze like a salamander shakes off its tail. She had completely forgotten that she had a baby, that she had to nurse it, change it, dress it. As the endless crying grew louder, the wounded mallard sitting in the middle of the living room trembled in agitation. Selma was no different from the mallard. As if a hand had ripped her from her natural habitat, imprisoned her in this dreadful house, and tied her down with the bonds of motherhood so she couldn't escape.

WHEN SHE WOKE UP IN THE MORNING, SHE CRAVED warm bread from a pit oven. Perhaps Songül had started the oven? Selma hadn't run into her in a while. She had only seen her once during her pregnancy; disgusted by her zeal to assist with the birth, she had done her best to avoid her after that. Once the baby was born, she had discouraged Yasin and Songül from visiting by acting cold. But this morning she realized that she missed watching Songül crouched by her oven, skillfully conquering the fire with her domesticity. Selma wanted to eat bread made with those practiced hands that infused all the foods they touched with earthy flavors.

She rose from her rumpled bed. She decided to take the children and pay a visit to Songül, hoping she would find her making bread by the pit oven.

When she saw Görkem curled up on one of the cushions in the living room, she quietly approached her daughter and woke her up with an unexpectedly loving voice. Görkem came to life like a flower in bloom. Selma's surprisingly soft voice met eyes that gleamed like sunbeams, and she smiled as if in a dream. Murat and the baby were sleeping in each other's arms on another cushion. Picking up the baby, Selma awakened Murat just as affectionately.

She said "Come along, kids, if we're lucky, Aunt Songül will have started the oven."

The children, accustomed to their mother's changeable temperament, often found it easier to cope with her melancholy than with her joy, which was like a snowglobe filled with sparkles that could settle any minute.

THE ROAD FROM THE TEACHER'S HOUSE TO THE VIL-lage stretched like a thin, clean line, as if cut by a razor blade across the Erciş Plateau. Selma, together with her happy, perplexed children, tried to make her way to the pit oven by following the footprints Yasin had left. When they got closer to the village, the sets of footprints multiplied, and the houses, painted in only a handful of colors, came into view. Soon they found themselves in a merry parade of sheep, goats, and geese that transformed them into characters from a fairy tale. Görkem and Murat, though clearly eager for some mischief, reined in their enthusiasm, since nothing in life terrified them like Selma's temper. They were like calves loosened from their tethers, ready to plunder everything in their path. Any outside observer could easily tell that they hadn't left home in a long time and were dulled by neglect.

Songül saw Selma and her children at a distance and ran toward them joyfully. Selma was also happy to see her. As they embraced one another, a warmth encircled the two. Before anyone asked, Songül said in a voice inflected with delight and a bit of resentment. "Let's head over to the pit oven; I just fired it to make bread." At that moment, nothing could have made Selma happier.

It was a sunny winter day. For the first time, the sun was facing the plains, warming the poplars, silverberries, and birches. The Erciş Plateau gleamed with snow crystals from end to end, the clouds over Mount Süphan had scattered, exposing its snowy peaks, while smoke issuing from village chimneys reached from the houses into the skies and flocks of starlings made their way toward the farmlands of neighboring villages. Songül ushered her long-absent friend and her children to the oven shed. As soon as they walked into the yard, a smell of ash struck Selma and the kids. Somehow, she felt neither like a mother nor like a guest, smiling with a sense of peace. Songül gathered them around the oven, pulled out cushions for them to sit.

Songül noticed the frailness of the infant that was laid on the cushion, when it wriggled itself out of the threadbare blanket that had been carelessly wrapped around it. She picked the baby up and inspected it with curiosity. She didn't like what she saw. She turned to Görkem and Murat, looked at them for a long while. The children were neglected, dirty, and, compared to when she last saw them, thinner. Görkem's cheeks that she remembered as perpetually pink had paled, her eyes were sunken, her skin dry. As if she was not a little girl but a mistreated house pet. Murat's arms, so thin, almost brittle, looked out of place on his body. The baby looked the worst. It exuded none of the fresh newborn energy, as if Selma had just dug it out of a grave, carelessly whisked off the dirt covering it, and brought it over to Songül without even bothering to dress it properly for the cold weather. It seemed that everything Yasin had told her was true.

She turned toward Selma, who was staring at the oven's fire with wonderment. Her madness—usually unnoticeable at first and evident only gradually—was reflected in Selma's demeanor, her gaze. Her eyes bulging, her hair unkempt, she was dressed in an odd assortment of clothes. Despite the arctic weather, she seemed perfectly comfortable in the flimsy cardigan she had thrown on.

She was so saddened by Selma's condition that for a while she didn't know what to say. Something was not right about Metin still being gone. Never in her life had Songül seen Selma, or for that matter anyone else, like this.

After a prolonged silence, Selma told Songül that the fire was almost out, and asked whether it wasn't time to make the bread. Songül had completely forgotten about the oven and the bread. Tearing herself away from her thoughts, she became her usual capable, enthusiastic self. She briskly pulled the pan of dough toward her, picked one of the balls she had rolled earlier and spread it on the bread peel. She reached into the oven all the way to her waist, and set the dough somewhere in the middle of the pit. She repeated this several times with the agile movements of a subterranean creature in her cave. Selma watched her, entranced, thinking how skillfully Songül dove in and out of the pit oven. Putting her weight on her knees, she swiftly thrust herself forward, her fat hips bouncing and settling each time, then plunged into the pit like a stone cast into the water.

As she watched Songül, she heard her children's giggles. They were stuffing themselves with steaming bread and herbed cheese.

By the time they were full, everything had calmed down, the children were drowsy with the heat, the sun had warmed the village and the entire plains.

Songül sat back, contented that she could satisfy both the bellies and the souls of her guests. She had baked her bread for the week, filled up her pan and covered it, setting some aside for Selma to take home.

With a wide smile, she picked the baby up in her arms and asked Murat his brother's name. He didn't know how to respond to this unexpected question. He glanced at Selma with dread. They were both quiet.

"He doesn't have a name, Aunt Songül."

Thinking that one should never take a child's word on serious matters, Songül pursed her lips comically and chided Murat "What a thing to say, you silly child; if you don't tell me, your sister will."

But before she could ask the same question, Görkem said, "Selma didn't name the baby."

Songül looked at Selma with a bewildered smile. When Selma said nothing, she became serious.

"Selma Hanım!" she said with a judging voice. "The baby is so frail, it will get sick; is your milk not enough?"

Selma didn't respond but shuffled her feet slightly to imply her displeasure.

"Görkem and Murat have also lost weight since I last saw them. And you're so pale. Are you ill? Are you alright, Selma Hanım?"

After an extended silence, she pressed "Where is our teacher? Where did he go? Do you know when he'll be back?"

When Selma didn't respond to any of her questions, Songül carefully swaddled the baby and passed it to its mother. "Take good care of your children, Selma Hanım. God forbid, if something were to happen to them, you'll be sad. Take especially good care of this baby; it's tiny, not strong enough, it'll get sick easily," she said.

Accepting the baby being handed to her, Selma stood up, signaling to her children with her eyes. They quickly pulled themselves together, and without waiting for their mother, they hurried out of the oven shed.

Selma smiled vaguely and thanked Songül for the bread, and set out after her children toward the lojman.

BACK IN THE HOUSE, THEY FELT EXHAUSTED, WIPED out by Songül's inquisitive gaze. Görkem took Murat to the duck, dragging him by the arm while Selma was brooding on Songül's tedious meddling with others' lives in the guise of honesty, benevolence, responsibility, and other drivel.

Songül couldn't conceal her secret pleasure as she gaped at the children with pity. She had disparaged Selma's motherhood to prove that she herself was the superior mother, which Selma found, in one word, repugnant. She was nothing more than a reptile who could never imagine loving herself. A hapless imbecile who could take pride simply in the existence of her children! And what to say about Yasin? Those peculiar glances of his that overpowered the other person with kindness! How she wished she could deliver him a blow and smash his brain and his benevolence.

The children had withdrawn to their usual corner and were playing with the duck. She calmed down when she saw them. She lay down next to the baby, on a cushion on the floor. She wrapped her weak arms around it and started nursing. When she was sure the infant had dozed off, she carried it to the bedroom, placing cushions all around the small body. She left the room quietly and went to the kitchen.

She set the warm bread on the kitchen counter and checked to see what there was to eat. Under the counter, there were potatoes, onions, lentils, and some tarhana. The pepper paste jar was empty but the oil would last them a while. As she stood in the kitchen, catatonic, not knowing what to do, she didn't notice Görkem come up to her. Görkem could tell that Selma wanted to cook but didn't have the strength for it. She took her mother's hand and led her to the stool by the wall. Looking into Selma's eyes with some affection and some hatred, she asked her how to cook.

Selma sighed as if a great weight had been lifted from her shoulders. Slowly, she began describing step by step how to chop the potatoes and the onions, how to rinse the lentils and cook them.

Görkem set the table. The weather had calmed; though the snow was everywhere, it felt like they had reached the end of a day left over from summer. Selma sat at the table, a maudlin expression on her face, and watched her daughter clumsily setting the plates on the table. After she finished arranging the table in her own fashion, Görkem took Nuniş with her and sat down. They started eating the unappetizing lentils at the unappealing table.

The wood stove slowly warmed the house, while at a distance, the tightly swaddled mallard sat next to two small dishes of water and wheat berries, waiting for its wounds to heal.

EYES LOVINGLY WATCHING THE MALLARD, A GRACE-ful murmur, caresses as gentle as the silky fragrances emanating from a silverberry... Selma! Selma! Resentment rose like a mountain! An earthquake of jealousy tore through Görkem's body.

As that creature so lacking in maternal love tended to the mallard with her sweet smiles, Görkem's eyes welled up. She wanted to destroy Selma, watch her fall into the clutches of a dreadful disease, even chew her between her own teeth.

Had Selma ever touched her the way she touched that bird? Had there ever been a day when her voice was as tender when speaking to her? Had she ever given her daughter a crumb of the attention she so generously doled out now? No! Never! None of this had ever happened. Görkem had never been captivated by the comforting gaze of a mother, had never experienced the swooning effect of a mother's love, never enjoyed that attention or inhaled that warm breath. Görkem had known none of this for the entire time she'd known herself. Selma attacked her daughter as if she'd taken an oath to seize everything that could ever make her happy. First, she took Metin, and now the mallard. Couldn't this piece of garbage exist without grabbing, without possessing? Greedy, vile traitor!

She wasn't going to allow it any longer. If the mallard wasn't hers, then she wouldn't be Selma's either.

She was going to avenge Metin's silence by taking the mallard back, and she was going to exact revenge for him too. She couldn't forget the day he and Selma had fought, and how, as he was walking out the door, Görkem had locked eyes with Metin. Selma had sat in a corner, soulless, lifeless like the books she never dropped from her hand, watching his departure with dead eyes. But now she would pay. When she realized that the duck she loved so generously would never belong to her, no amount of remorse would save her, her pleas would fall on deaf ears, she would be denied any mercy. Selma was the source of a fire that burned in the middle of a serene lake, a fire she stubbornly reignited with a splash of gasoline every time it died out. If she had polluted the wellspring of that crystal clear water, then she was going to pay for what she had done.

"WHY DID YOU DO THIS?"

Görkem was looking at the mallard, whose head she had severed from its body. Her hands were covered in blood up to her wrists. She had pressed the animal's head against her belly and ripped it off; she was still reeling with the euphoria of her deed. Selma looked at her heaving chest, her rosy nose in the first light of day, her bloodied locks, her motionless lips. The way she grasped death with her hands, the way she defied everything she was ever taught to the point of madness, rendered this child inscrutable to Selma.

"Why did you do this?"

Görkem responded without turning her head, "I want the summer to come; I want to get away from here with Teacher Mahir. Everything is so boring, Selma!"

Weary, Selma sat down on a chair near them. "We talked this over so many times, Teacher Mahir is dead. Someone killed him and dumped him in the ravine. Don't you remember? He's never coming back!"

Ignoring Görkem's silence, she went on.

"Go bury that animal in the snow. I'll clean the rug. You clean up your clothes. I don't want to hear your whining anymore."

Görkem picked up the duck's body from the floor. She was happy. Selma had lost the battle. Görkem had managed to rock her throne.

The sun shone bright enough to scorch the plains, were it not for the winter. The brilliant light, the trembling sunrays blinded Görkem. She marched victoriously. From the corner of her eye, she looked at the mallard in her hands. The blood smeared on its bill had dried. Its belly resembled a deflated ball. She was flooded with the indescribable exhilaration she had experienced when she had ripped off Nuniş's arm. Now the bird looked the way she wanted. Unlike everything else in nature, it was imperfect, incongruous and anomalous. The expression on her face softened. She didn't have the heart to bury the body in the snow. Besides, she didn't have to do everything Selma told her.

She wondered what to do instead. She wanted to take the mallard back home, but she knew she'd get in trouble if Selma found out that she hadn't buried it. Maybe when Selma wasn't looking, she'd sneak the bird inside the house and hide it somewhere. Questions and schemes clashed with each other in her head when, in the distance, she noticed Yasin coming. She panicked momentarily. In all likelihood, he was coming to check on the flag. First, he'd walk up to the flagpole, and if he decided something was not right, he'd come and talk to Selma and fix it. Görkem looked at the pole. The flag was wrapped around it again. She hurried toward the house before Yasin got any closer.

THE PART OF THE SKY VISIBLE FROM THE WINDOW was depressing. The clouds had grown dark, packed in clusters. It was unlikely that the sun would show its face. The neglected plants shriveling on the windowsill summed up the despondency inside the lojman in all its starkness. Selma's fingers trailed along the houseplants; she didn't belong in the landscape surrounding her. She tried to erase herself from the entire picture. Closing her eyes, she imagined herself as a hideous creature who had accidentally stumbled into the earth's photograph. She could see everything more clearly when she had her eyes closed: worthless souls out of place in every landscape, rabid microorganisms among the flower petals, the eerie discordance between children and the sky. . . . Haphazardly, she tore the dry leaves from one of the plants, and as she crumbled them in her palm, she opened her eyes and met Görkem's gaze, a reminder of the recent devastation, right by her side. She shuddered. The crushed leaves in her hand made her uneasy. Hiding her hand behind her back, she asked her daughter what she wanted. Görkem would have uttered a few words to say that she was hungry, but she knew this would move Selma less than a feather could a move a wall.

She turned around, walking toward Murat and the baby. She wasn't hungry anymore. Selma's icy stare had taken care of that, and when she saw the raw, gnawed potato in Murat's hand, she lost her appetite altogether. She crawled under the covers, aware that what she had done a few days ago was murder, that she had killed the mallard in cold-blood. She pressed her head into the pillow, taking refuge inside a cocoon. She knew her mother wouldn't protect her from anything that overwhelmed her; on the contrary, she would sacrifice her for her own sins.

A LUMINOUS MORNING. SNOW ON THE EARTH'S SUR-
face, summery clouds in the sky. Glowing, soft, tufted like
sheep's wool, clear outlines . . .

Görkem was stretched out, practically unconscious among
the disarray in the middle of the living room. Hunger had overtaken her body, and was scraping at the walls of her stomach like
an impertinent guest.

A mysterious odor had permeated the house. Selma, frown-
ing with disgust, was searching for its source. Perplexed, she
stepped over Görkem's body and continued looking around her.
Bad odors always irked her. Suspecting that the children might
have peed somewhere in the house, her eyes sought out Murat,
who had fallen asleep on the armchair. Waking him up with an
impulsive jerk, she asked "Do you smell something, son?" Picking at his crusty eyes with his fingers, Murat tried to pull himself together. Selma got hold of her rage, and through clenched
teeth, whispered at Murat.

"Where's this odor coming from?"

"I don't know."

"There's an odor; don't you smell it?"

Noticing the menacing oscillations of her mother's voice, Görkem spoke up, "No, Selma. I don't smell anything bad either."

"How do you know it's bad then? I said there's an odor. I didn't say there's a bad odor."

"I don't know."

"Answer me straight. So you can smell a bad odor!"

"I don't know."

"Am I stupid, Görkem?"

"No, Selma."

"Then why aren't you giving me a straight answer?"

"I don't know."

"What do you not know?"

"I'm starving, Selma."

"God forgive me, girl! Answer me, where is this odor coming from?"

"I don't know!"

"Murat, do you smell it, son?"

"No, mommy."

The interrogation ended abruptly. Silence descended. The mysterious bad odor blanketed the silence.

Selma waited. When the silence reached the threshold of her forbearance, she started yelling.

"Aren't you two smelling this? Answer me, Murat! Child, I'm talking to you! Speak, son! Speak, you dog! You stupid dog!"

It was like an explosive device had blasted unexpectedly in the middle of a peaceful gathering. Murat lost his color; the giant, coarse brush of his mother's words painted his countenance white. His eyes grew wide with the terror of the imminent threat. As his saliva balled itself into a small pearl in his throat, two clouds of sorrow descended on his shoulders. He was confused, frightened. For the first time in his brief life, he was witnessing his own heart breaking.

Selma never called her children names or cursed at them. This was a first. No matter how enraged she might be, insults, swear words never issued from her lips. But this time, something had changed. She had lost control, failed to rein in her temper.

So, this was how far the lojman had destroyed their relationships. The secret tissue that held them together was diseased at its core. As the tissue broke, damaged, rotting cells surfaced, oozing a black fluid, threatening the implacable web of knots that kept them in place.

Görkem was surprised by what she'd heard, too, but she knew that she'd rattled her mother's nerves, disturbed her unperturbable solemnity, and deep down she roared with victory cries. Profanities had escaped Selma's lips so clumsily, so crudely that, had she repeated them, Görkem would have burst into a hoot of laughter. She could never have imagined that Selma would sound so ridiculous, so foolish.

THE SKY CHANGED IN WAVES OF LIGHT: CHESTNUT, red, yellow. Trying with a superhuman effort to keep her eyes open, Selma watched the clouds thinning, drifting apart. Her back turned to the house, to everything that had happened, she stood by the window, lost in the panorama of Lake Van bathed in cascades of light. There were almost-fossilized footprints on the snow, giving Selma the sense that winter would last forever, that she would spend the rest of her life in this ice desert.

It was almost dusk. The days were so short that Selma was taken aback when night arrived. Time flew by in the blink of an eye; how did everything that happened manage to squeeze itself into that interval?

After several hours, she still hadn't been able to identify the source of the odor, and though she had resorted to opening the window, she couldn't escape it. It was unpleasant, sharp enough to cut at her nerve endings. It besieged her like an invisible curtain, seeped inside her with every breath, oppressing her lungs. She looked in every corner, under the cushions, beside the bookshelf, among the toys, behind the television, inside the bed and the wardrobe, in the chest where she kept the bedding, around the kitchen. She could barely keep herself from ripping apart all the furniture in the house.

Perhaps she ought to identify what the odor resembled. Names of things that would produce foul smells poured from her lips as if she was hallucinating them. Strangely, she realized she was not skillful enough to distinguish between odors. What exactly did rotten vegetables smell like? Or feces, sweat, or corpses. Vomit and rancid food couldn't smell the same. She pressed her fingers against her forehead and rubbed her skin. Her pupils dilated; she had to hold her nose to keep herself from throwing up. She thought of corpses, food, feces, vomit. The smell of putrefaction. Sweet pastry smells, perfumes, animals . . .

GÖRKEM PRESSED THE ROTTING MALLARD TO HER chest. Its smell comforted her. She felt dizzy, her eyelids slowly closed. Sighs were followed by quick, abrupt hip movements. Holding the severed head of the mallard in one hand, she stroked, scrubbed, jabbed at herself with the rotting body. Her nostrils flared, her chest tightened with pleasure.

She imagined her mother, she pictured her face blood-red with rage.

She shrieked, louder and louder, hoping to attract Selma's attention. Tearing off her clothes, she pressed the mallard harder into her body. She rubbed the carcass against her indistinct nipples, against her navel, her head, her neck. She swung the severed head, now pounding it on the floor now raising it toward the ceiling, transforming herself into a satanic musician in an imaginary orchestra. Finally, she succeeded in scaring awake the baby, whom Selma had forgotten. If she didn't bother to leave her bed despite all of Görkem's screaming and bellowing, perhaps she would be overcome by motherhood's sensitive conscience and make her appearance in the living room, unable to resist the cries of the earthworm she had birthed. Feverish with excitement, Görkem rolled her body in bed. Like an animal in heat, she shook, she trembled; the more she yelled, the louder the baby cried. She thrust her body back and forth, her knees began bleeding, she continued her spectacle until she was hoarse from screaming. The mallard's carcass was in pieces. Selma didn't stir. Neither her bellowing nor the heart-wrenching cries of the baby had worked. She lay in her bed like a slab of ice. She heard, saw, felt nothing, she was immovable.

The baby, drained from crying, lingered between sleep and exhaustion, while Görkem lay dazed on the floor, the mallard's carcass and head in her lap, her finger inside its eye socket. The lojman swallowed all that had happened, casting the absurd savagery down into the insentient wells of eternity, normalizing everything.

THE SOURCE OF THE SMELL HAD FINALLY BEEN revealed. The face that had concealed it under cushions, under piles of dirty clothes, now stood before her, casting glances that signaled she was proud of her work. Selma looked away; the last thing she wanted right now was to be dragged into a new losing battle.

Perhaps, the truth was that she felt too tired to flare up and roar in anger. She had no strength left to cope with the schemes of her daughter who struggled so hard to make her existence visible, trying to ensnare and suffocate her inside this existence. The more she tried to free herself, the more trapped she felt, spewing venom into life, the lojman, the world. If only Metin were with her. He used to resolve such skirmishes before they became problems and keep the children in balance. He had a knack for taking care of minor troubles easily. Ever since he'd left, the house had fallen out of its orbit. The children were nothing like their usual selves. Something had happened to her, too. She felt weak, listless; whatever it was that had reduced her to this unbearable state, where the first spark had come from, she didn't know. "Oh, Metin! Why aren't you here? Where are you?" As the words fell from her lips, she began to cry. Her tears were warm, they trickled down her cheeks and into her mouth, where they mixed with her saliva. She sighed while her eyes wandered to the school's flagpole. Absentmindedly, for no reason . . . Just like staring at the bleak landscape.

The flag wasn't up. Surprised that the week was already over, Selma ventured into studying the rusted iron post. It shot straight up, as if intent on wounding the sky. Days, weeks, months went by, all sorts of things happened to them, yet the pole stood exactly where it stood. The flag was raised every Monday by Yasin, and lowered every Friday by Yasin. Deaths, births, migrations, winter, nothing disturbed this routine. In the face of everything, this stupid pole stood defiantly erect right there, and she couldn't stand it. Someone had to have declared it the symbol of misfortune, indescribable agonies, and nightmares. Yasin, the keeper of the ritual, kept exalting and exalting it. She clenched her teeth. Did she have to sacrifice herself to end this black curse? The more she thought the deeper she got sucked into a well of meaninglessness, of nothingness.

She called Görkem.

Her daughter approached with drowsy steps. She was standing by the bird carcass like an indestructible monument, her index finger, slightly bent, solemnly pointing to it.

It had been clear from the start that stuffing the mallard in the pile of dirty clothes was a bad idea. But, in this tiny house, it wasn't easy for anyone to hide their misdeeds. Besides, it was difficult to move the corpse every single day. What she feared had finally happened. Selma loomed above the carcass, demanding a confession.

Looking into her daughter's frightened, bewildered eyes, she told her to take the mallard and throw it outside. Her punishment was just that. Selma wasn't going to do anything else. She didn't feel like it. All she wanted was to be rid of the corpse immediately.

Görkem would have preferred a beating or a scolding instead of this punishment. Her eyes welling with tears, she walked toward the carcass. The mallard's head lay next to Nuniş. She stared at them for a moment. Maybe she could keep the mallard's head at least? Leaning down, she cradled the mallard in her arms, as if afraid of hurting it. The carcass still thrilled her, despite everything.

She decided to place the mallard among the wet firewood. Why hadn't she thought of hiding it in the coal shed earlier? Selma wouldn't have been able to find her plaything there. She rarely went into the coal shed, mostly saddling Görkem with the task.

Just as she was about to lay a few more logs over the mallard and walk out of the shed, she decided that the head didn't look right at all next to the body. Thinking further, she concluded that she wasn't going to save the head. In this, the strangest, the most memorable event in her short life, she must destroy the details that could disturb her. Gingerly, she bent over, cupped the mallard's head, and pressed her cheek against the beautiful, iridescent green feathers. Resting cheek to cheek, she remained like that for a long time. This thing, nature's most exalted creation, had no place in the world of the living. She seized upon a natural way to bid farewell to such a beauty. She crushed the affection she felt for the head she was holding in her hands and tossed it out the window. After placing a few more pieces of firewood over the body, she set out for the house. She walked on the snow as if walking on clouds. As if the earth was slipping from under her feet. She could almost take wing; her heart nearly stopped. She had defeated Selma again; what Görkem wanted had happened, not what Selma had ordered. No matter what she did, Selma couldn't take away her plaything.

Selma saw her come in through the door and could tell from her demeanor that she had been up to something. She was actually charmed by that small, sweet face that was clearly putting on an act. Silly worm! How she strutted, so self-assured. Now, she was in the bedroom, now in the living room, now in the kitchen. Moving anxiously, breathlessly scanning around, she had no idea that Selma was aware of everything. She could see the war that Görkem had knowingly and willingly declared against her. But she had neither the weapons nor the time to defeat her. Never mind fighting Görkem, she didn't even have the stamina to contend with herself.

She watched Görkem pull Nuniş out from between the cushions. She was already quite old to be playing with a doll. At an age when she could be expanding the reach of her intellect, she insisted on treading water. The gray, bleak lojman where nothing changed, didn't even allow for the illusion of change anymore; seasons changed, children grew, flocks of birds blended with the landscape, and yet, all that was left was the bitter, familiar taste of repetition.

II

WAS THERE STILL A WORLD OUTSIDE? SHE COULDN'T
tell. She could not perceive the familiar sounds and smells, the
infinite landscape that usually animated her desires and spoke to
her senses. If there ever had been a world, or the possibility of a
world, it must be far away now—retreated, erased, lost. Time had
come loose, the past and the future torn from their roots, jum-
bled, pulped into a menacing present.

Emptiness nestled in her chest cavity, widening to fill it. With
her eyes closed, she listened to the tones emerging from between
her ribs. She held her breath and waited, not wanting to miss
a single note of the swelling sound. It grew louder, becoming
solid, palpable, erupting through her skin, saturating her surroundings. Pulsating beats lifted her body, and she was hurled
on a wave of sound, ending up in a corner of the living room.

Something viscid struck her face. With that contact, the buzz-
ing that had been gathering inside her chest turned to revulsion.

When she tried pushing her legs down and away from her
stomach, she felt them tearing through something that was
malleable, but very dense. She could barely move; her entire
body was being kneaded by a wet, slimy dough. Solid, palpable,

pressing against her hands, her feet, her face. Her pores opened, her skin stretched and contracted, as if struggling to adapt to a new life form. She waited inside that unnameable, terrifying sensation. The horrible texture was touching every part of her. Her body tensed, her hair bristled, and she was seized with fear of this experience she could not define.

Warily, she opened her eyes, and her eyeballs instantly felt a cool pressure against them, accompanied by a burning sensation, slight and short-lived. Now she could see the substance that enveloped her: translucent, light gray in color, made of a dense, supple material.

The substance hadn't just swallowed her, it was impeding her movement. Its squeeze was unrelenting. She wanted to rub her eyes, but couldn't lift her arm to bring her hand to her face. How strange that she could not perform such a simple motion. Unconvinced, she tried again, but failed. She flailed in panic. But her efforts amounted to no more than squirming in place, like a fly in a spiderweb, awaiting its executioner. She paused and tried to understand. She had been engulfed by something, paralyzed. What was this? Was she in a dream? What was happening?

She felt her shoulders contract, her feet flex, her stomach, her intestines deflate. Her brow was drenched in sweat. How long had she been inside this thing? When did this start? Had it been like this for a long time?

She must hold her mouth tightly shut, she thought. She didn't want to let the strange substance enter her body. Her eyes scanned the walls, the doors, the windows, looking for a way out, a crack, a hole to escape through. But could it be that the world offered her no escape? Was this the most it would ever be, some thing that swallowed her whole, body and will, like an uncontainable deluge of obligations? Whatever it was, the substance had filled every nook and cranny. She tried to tear, punch, kick through it, but nothing worked. It would not budge, tear, or break. Her mind raced from thought to thought, her heart beating as if it would burst through her chest. Out of breath, exhausted, she stopped fighting, decided to rest a while, to wait.

Gradually she calmed herself, convinced that she was having a dream. She strained to open her eyes fully. With great exertion, she was able to move her head to the right and then left. And despite everything, she could still breathe.

A second wave of panic overcame her, and she began thrashing her arms and legs, but all she managed was to push her body slightly higher up. For endless minutes she remained there, motionless, weightless. Her stomach began to churn with a bitter sensation akin to nausea. She closed her mouth even tighter, swallowing her saliva in the attempt to tamp down the sour taste.

She tried to move herself down toward the floor by flapping her feet as forcefully as she could, but found she couldn't make use of her body weight, as if she were suspended by an invisible rope.

One shouldn't come to this world in the first place, she thought; one shouldn't be born, shouldn't love or become attached. Attachments gave way to incomplete, warped relationships, cords you couldn't cut or tear yourself away from. That pale gray, gelatinous thing took hold of you right where you held onto life; those vague hopes, those accursed, conciliatory thoughts creating the illusion that there may be a place for you on earth, a place of your own that you could paint in colors of your choosing.

NOW SHE SAW GÖRKEM ACROSS THE ROOM. SHE looked startled, scared, frozen in the corner with Nuniş in her hand. Her arms were stretched out, her chest appeared wider, her hair was a tousled mess. Judging from the way her eyes darted from side to side, studying the substance that had descended upon her, she seemed at least as terrified as Selma herself. There was such a mournful expression on her face that Selma's heart ached for her. It was upsetting to see her daughter that way, though she was glad to find she was not alone.

After a while, her eyes sought out Murat and the baby. They were nowhere to be seen. Her heart began to race with unfamiliar feelings. Small grunting sounds escaped her nostrils like the squealing of an underwater creature echoing in the ocean; she wanted to call out, but failed.

She tried to focus on her breathing to calm herself. She could die of panic. She counted her breaths. One, two, three . . . She repeated the numbers over and over, waiting to awaken from the nightmare.

Her effort seemed to work, and she convinced herself that she would wake up shortly. Murat had gone to the bedroom to sleep. She vividly recalled the moment. In pajamas that were too short for him, with his ever-brooding eyes, his face buried in silence, his head lowered, he had walked to the bedroom. She could picture the way he walked so clearly that she was relieved, if only a little.

She noticed that she was worried more for her children than for herself, and this was an alien feeling. She was losing the distance she had worked to establish between herself and her children, the stubborn indifference she'd been building up for years. She searched for the baby, trying to turn her head, stirring with difficulty. As she wrestled with her mounting anxiety, she spotted the baby's scrawny body suspended slightly above the floor. In a deep slumber, it appeared peaceful, content, its lips swollen, eyelids softly closed. A rosy, wholesome, sleep-induced beauty tiptoed across its cheeks.

Solace. What wouldn't she give to find a way to tear herself from this nightmare and return to that old, familiar, ordinary farce she hadn't been able to bear waking up to each day.

THE ERCİŞ PLATEAU LAY UNDER SNOW. WINTER WAS extending its dominion. Everyone had withdrawn into their houses, the village was forgotten, even by its denizens. Flocks of mallards no longer merged into the sky's scenery, nor rested in the hot springs, their calls hadn't been heard since they left the plains. Yasin had been wandering—sometimes calmly, sometimes nervously—through the snow-covered, lifeless streets, the reedbeds near the lake, the beet fields and frozen water canals, looking for a sign of Metin. At times, he dreaded finding what he was looking for, then sometimes he would forget, and then, a knot would settle in his throat because he knew all too well what he would find.

He had last seen Metin walking the village road toward the asphalt. A melancholy aura about him, his tall frame swaying like the poplars in the wind. Yet his footsteps were decisive, yielding to the natural elements with a self-assured sense of acceptance. When Yasin saw him from a distance, Metin had looked like someone who wanted to leave everything behind, who would never return. Yasin had wanted to run after him, stop him, calm him down, but he couldn't do it.

It was almost two months since Metin had vanished. Yasin didn't dare walk to the township. The winter had been harsher than ever. God forbid if he were to become stranded, freeze to death. Who would take care of his family? He wouldn't leave unless he could trust the weather.

Selma and the children worried him. Selma had lost control of her mental faculties, more so than usual. She wasn't taking care of her children, left them to fend for themselves without even feeding them. If it went on like this, her newborn could die. Worse yet, she allowed neither Songül nor Yasin to intervene. Gradually, she had cut off all her ties with them. He was not even allowed to raise and lower the flag anymore.

Gazing into the distance with helpless grief—was there really nothing he could do for Metin's family?—he resolved not to abandon Selma and the children, no matter what. When Metin showed up, he shouldn't find his family all alone, with no one caring for them; he should know that Yasin had not just left them to their fate. No matter what Selma said or thought, Yasin knew Metin had entrusted his family to him. If only for the children's sake, he was going to check in on them, to see if they were eating or not. The fear of failing his friend grated at his heart; he was going to knock on their door every single day.

He was hungry. Tired, too. He tried to think of nothing but the meal Songül was preparing. That morning by the pit oven, she had mentioned she was going to make keledos stew. Surely, she would serve rice and herbed cheese with it. The thought stimulated his appetite. He was overcome by an irrepresible desire for both the meal and for Songül. He smiled, a wave of warmth radiating from his neck to his cheeks. He headed for home.

GÖRKEM TRIED STRETCHING TO RID HERSELF OF THE
sense of being trapped. With some difficulty, she was able to
move her head, her hands, her feet. She was frightened, trembling, her eyes opened so wide it seemed they might burst from
their sockets. She perceived that she was suspended inside a
dreadful, suffocating substance, like a naked lightbulb dangling
from the ceiling. She waited for someone to come to her aid.
As she wiggled her toes, she noticed that the substance engulf-
ing her was, despite its density, elastic. Trapped inside a nightmare, she thought. Would that ghoulish bag of bones from her
dreams pop out of thin air and come for her again? But when
had she even fallen asleep? Had she not just hidden the mallard
in the coal shed, come back inside the house, and even felt Selma's interrogating eyes upon her as soon as she walked into the
living room? She remembered everything precisely, but no matter how much she tried, she couldn't remember the moment she
had fallen asleep. She turned her head with curiosity. Oh, there!
She saw Selma. She felt a sense of relief, quickly followed by
anger. What was Selma doing in her dream? She was like pars-
ley, tossed into every dish! Selma was suspended too, and, like

her own, Selma's eyes were wide. Her neck was flushed, veins bulging, and she looked frightening. Her mouth pursed, she was staring at Görkem. Was she pleading for help or was she about to help her; her body language was so confusing that Görkem couldn't tell. Selma stood like a rootless tree, its fruit plundered. Her loneliness had transformed her into a sad, pitiful statue. Lonely and despicable Selma! Görkem turned away, not wanting to look at her.

She kept her mouth tightly closed. Like Selma, she was afraid of swallowing this substance she could not identify. They both hung motionless in the goo like two figurines glazed with sadness. Although Görkem was convinced she was having a bad dream, she couldn't stop herself from trembling in fear. Despite the annoyance of her mother being in her dream, she was worried that the bag of bones would show up any minute. And if that ghoulish demon were to appear, she wouldn't be able to overcome her fear unless Selma held her. Without thinking, she tried moving closer to Selma, whose face revealed all too clearly that she had gone completely mad. Stupid woman! Just look at her, she thought to herself, just like a fly on on a pile of horse dung. No one could convince her that she was Selma's daughter. How could such a selfish, callous woman possibly be her mother? They didn't even look alike. Selma's eyebrows were light and thin, hers dark and thick. Görkem had large eyes and a deep gaze, but Selma's beady eyes were so small that most of the time you couldn't even tell where she was looking. Her nose was ugly, too. Selma's fingers, short, stubby; Görkem's, long and slender. Not a single feature in common. Neither their dispositions nor their looks were the same. A look, a gesture. Anything at all . . . Nothing!

She continued to study her. The result was a fiasco, as always. Selma failed to evoke even the slightest positive sentiment in Görkem. Neither admiration nor love . . . She had turned her dream into a nightmare, just as she had ruined her life. What was she, beyond an unfeeling, useless wretch, forever at war with her maternal instincts? If only Selma would die. If only something could put an end to her breathing. Soon, she would wake up to a reality in which everything worked out in Selma's favor. No way to escape the inevitable, her hands would be tied, and the world would once again revolve around Selma. Why did no one ever ask her whether she wanted to be Selma's child? Why did she have to sprout inside the belly of this crazy woman? Why couldn't she even escape her in her dream?

When she interrupted her brooding, she noticed that she had not moved. What a long dream this was. Both she and Selma hovered in the middle of the room. She wanted to throw out her arms, kick this way and that, but couldn't. Her body would budge by a few centimeters at most, before it was pulled back, like she was glued in place. Her eyes filled with desperate tears. Keeping her mouth shut tight, she broke into sobs.

FEELING REMORSE ABOUT EVERYTHING SHE'D DONE
in her life, Selma squirmed in agony and despair. This nightmare
had been chasing her for years, biding its time until it finally
pounced and captured her.

Had she never come to this village, never entered this house,
maybe none of this would have happened. If only she had gone
after Metin when he left. If only she had taken his hand and left
everything behind. She had entered this prison with them as if
she was obligated. Wretched vampires, filthy maggots . . . Just
like shadows made visible by sunlight, they were exposed in her
thoughts for the bloodsuckers they were. She didn't want them,
at the very least, not in her dream. She saw her own ruin in their
faces, she watched herself disintegrate like a statue made of salt.
As soon as she woke up from her dream she was going to leave
the three of them to starve, she would clear out without even
looking back. For the time being, she could do nothing. Nothing but wait for Metin to come back. Perhaps, when she awakened from her dream, Metin would be back, and he would wrap
his arms around her. He would gently raise her from where she
lay with sweet kisses and his warm breath. She would surrender

herself to that tight embrace, everything would return to normal, for better or for worse, to its own rhythm. Her heart tightened with longing and regret. How had she managed to say all those harsh words to Metin? How could she hurt him so, given his sincerity, his kindness? She'd kept insulting him, even after she saw his face turn pale. She was angry with herself. She had acted childishly, not like a mature woman. She'd been stubborn, like a fool born without the proper share of reason. Of course Metin was right not to forgive her, but he had to come back now. As much as Selma needed him, he needed her, and his children.

Metin, wake me up, please wake me up from this nightmare. Give me a chance to make amends.

THE BABY LOOKED GLOSSY AND FRAGILE, LIKE PORCE-
lain. Despite an urge to destroy it with one small blow, Görkem
looked over at its palms, the rosy skin between its fingers. Its sweet
twitches while it slept were spine-chilling. Since the day it was
born, her sibling had failed to win her over. It was a disgusting
slug. Soft, doughy, it begged to be chewed on. How unnerving to
know that soon it would start waddling around. Those feet that
were on the verge of walking, she wanted to crush them, cripple
them, rip them from its legs if she could. If she ever woke up from
this dream, the first thing would be to slice off its toes one by one
at their skinny joints. Caught in a wave of hatred, she hurled herself toward the baby. The goo thwarted her leap and snapped her
back in place.

Where was her best friend, her true brother? She hadn't seen
him in this dream. He would usually be by her side. Even Selma
was in her dream, but not her brother. And worse, this nightmare dragged on and on, like the winter, becoming something
inescapable. The snow, the cold, and the dream . . . All three held
her in place, kept her from moving far away; they sentenced her
to Selma, slowly killing her. She wanted the winter to end, for

the hot summer days to arrive, for Teacher Mahir to return to the village. Even if Selma didn't like him, she would always love Mahir.

This was the best punishment she could hand her mother.

No Selma, no baby, no winter, no dream . . . None of them mattered. She was alone with the dizzying bliss of thinking about him. She had been called by love; she had been embraced by love. In her short life she had been granted one and only one treasure; no one could touch it. It comforted her like a prayer before sleep, magical. She imagined herself in her beloved's arms, nestled like a squirrel against his tall body. His heartbeats rippled throughout the goo. She was excited to sense all around her the stirrings of his noisy intestines, the quiet agitation of his stomach and chest. What happiness, what an indescribable peace this was. Teacher Mahir's warm and talkative body could make her forget about the winter, the cold, the nightmare. As if looking down into the mouth of a well, she looked into his eyes, the irises speckled with soft shades of brown. She wrapped her scrawny arms around his waist. She moved her nose along his chest, his groin, places where she could inhale his smell. Like a timid insect, she weaved around his neck, his waist, his legs. Between shivers of affection and passion, she pressed her lips to Teacher Mahir's lips, like warm morsels of pastry. All her questions were answered, she had come to an understanding with the world.

WINDSTORM, FROST . . . WINTER WILL NEVER END, flowers will never bloom, birdsong will never return.

That man in love, that body of boundless trust is no more. The skin melting under a hot gaze, the soul stoked by exclamations of delight, the probing, attentive caresses will not return. These were the thoughts going through Selma's mind as the world became even more appalling. She remembered with an aching heart the day they moved into the lojman. How she had despised the cheerful way Metin carried in the suitcases. She had already sensed how the gray walls would eclipse the scenic landscape, eventually contaminating even their inner landscapes, and that they would be forgotten by everyone just like dry, waterless wells. Yet, how hopeful Metin's eyes had been that day. Far from worried, he was joyous. Weightless, like the clouds gathered over the mountaintops. He was drunk with the landscape stretching out toward the beet fields. He was unaware that one day this house he looked upon with such hopeful eyes would turn his and Selma's hearts to concrete.

And the day she first saw her husband, that first moment when she spied him chatting with his friends by the wall that encircled the campus . . . Wearing an unremarkable pair of jeans, a blue tee-shirt, sneakers. Holding in his hands—she would come to find out—a book of poetry. As she got to know Metin, she discovered his passion for poetry, which excited her. Like her, he too was lost in verses. How could she have known that she was to fall in love with this enthusiastic youth who was talking to his friends with his broad smile, that she would marry him and have children with him.

When Metin graduated from university and was assigned his first post as a teacher, they didn't have the slightest inkling of their misfortune. During their most creative years, they would be dragged from post to post, perpetually moving from one town to another. Making things worse, they had brought into the world three children, crowning their misfortune with their own hands. The fights that began with Görkem's birth grew like a landslide, turning Selma and Metin into strangers. All that was left of the wreckage of those enchanted moments were the grayness of the lojman and the children's selfish, incessant demands. The grayness and the children had put an end to the nights of poetry, clouded their amorous gazes. Their glow extinguished, they were left entirely helpless. Before that, the devil could still tempt them, tear them away from all that was sacred and flood their souls with chaos. They had been scorched with love, with pleasure; they had fed on the fruits of the most exalted of sins. But, god and the lojman had blindfolded the devil with the gossamer tulle of monotony; they had destroyed the lord of that golden era, the guardian of poetry and genitals.

Her eyes lingered on the breathtaking landscape of the Erciş Plateau. Black clouds descended upon the reedbeds, joining the fears growing inside her. Inside the goo, she was a captive deprived of the devil, poetry, love; a nobody; she was no on eat all, perhaps less than nothing.

WITH ALL HER STRENGTH, SHE TRIED TO MOVE IN the direction of the door. If only she could touch it, the door would open and she could make her escape. She flailed her feet, her arms as if swimming. She had to grab hold of something. She pushed herself to the limits of her strength but she still couldn't budge even a centimeter. In that maddening helplessness, her confidence crumbled; it seemed the goo had seized not just her body but also her spirit, her mind. She wanted nothing more than to be able to press one hand to her heart and weep. Or, at least to be able to lean her head against something. Yet, hovering in space like this, trapped and struggling, she couldn't perform the slightest movement that might give her a physical or mental boost to experience a sense of peace.

She was about to burst with frustration. She had to think to preoccupy herself, to seek refuge in times when she had felt good. Nothing pleasant other than her husband came to mind.

Oh, Metin! They wore you down; I wasn't understanding toward you. Come back now. Sing songs into my ear, dissolve this goo that embalms my body.

Selma's chin trembled. She remembered the poems Metin had recited with closed eyes. His gentle face, his childlike voice. She pictured those moments when he went straight from her embrace to traipsing about in the living room, looking like he was one of god's angels. As he tore away from their lovemaking with a small curtsy of sentimentality, she would feel wonder that he still had so much to tell her, and find his bashful nudity amusing.

She shook with chilling sadness when she recalled how Metin had embraced this village to which he'd been banished, and how much, despite everything, against all her complaints, he had hoped to make her appreciate it.

"They banished us to the pit of hell, Metin!"

"No, Selma, this landscape is a piece of paradise."

"We're in the middle of nowhere, just a mountain and us, Metin, can't you see?"

"Yes, Mount Süphan!"

"I hate your stupidity, Metin!"

"I love everything about you, sweet darling!"

She smiled. Her longing swelled. She wanted her lover by her side. She kept her love like an extravagant noun in a secret corner of her heart. She waited for the day when he would end the absolute inner silence; she watched for Metin's return to revive that exuberant desire. Waiting had gifted her with a vast darkness that only steeled her spirit. Now, all she wanted was to forsake her children, the house, her halo of melancholy, and go far away, alone with her lover. Her mind could still invoke a luminous image of Metin to obliterate the endless desert of discontent that spread across her geography of inner peace.

Could misfortune explain all that had happened? To a faithless person, how convincing, how reassuring would it be to explain a world through misfortune?

Had she ever known anything other than sadness in this endless journey of life? Had they told her anything other than the lie that she would walk through bright green meadows?

The questions fell on her head like giant boulders breaking off from the mountains. As she sighed, thinking that Metin could hear her, she said out loud: "Just the two of us! Let's go."

TIME'S IMPERVIOUS WEDGE. THE VILLAGE BOLTED IN place. Destiny's horizon narrowed, the jinn of happenstance slipping into spaces that belong to human beings. Unruly elements, the causes behind events.

Finished with his chores at the stable, he lay down, exhausted, on the living room floor of the the mud brick house. He waited for Songül to set the table. His children were beside him, sitting quietly. The oldest had started high school the year before, the youngest was in first grade.

The cold weather offered Yasin no chance to go to the township. For months, the storms hadn't subsided, nor had the sun shown its face much. Since the day Metin vanished, the weather had become more brutal. He had talked to the village muhtar a few times; he had wanted to alert the gendarmes, but couldn't do anything because the phone lines were down. His hands were tied. Who could defy winter?

From the corner of his eye, he looked at his children and was overcome by love. He proudly admired their resemblance to him. When his hunger became unbearable, he called out to his wife. Songül hurried to set the dinner tray on the floor. Lentil soup, potato stew, rice, ayran, and herbed cheese. As he ate, his disquiet returned when Songül asked about Metin. Morsels swelled in his mouth. He felt helpless.

Songül—in fact, the entire village—expected him to find Metin. Why was no one but Yasin out looking for him? Selma Hanım herself hadn't made a single attempt to find her husband, and why did everyone expect this of him? Was it because Yasin was closer to him than anyone else? How strange! After all, he was the village teacher and he had been gone for weeks. It was simply cruel that they put all the responsibility on his shoulders when everyone ought to be doing their part to find him.

Try as he did to chase away his thoughts, he noticed the weary lines on Songül's face. She was exhausted by the endless winter, the children's incessant whining, the chores that multiplied; her large, hazel eyes had sunken in. When she saw that her husband was lost in thought while staring at her, she asked Yasin what was bothering him. To evade what he was really thinking, he brought up Selma.

"Go check on Selma Hanım today."

Disinclined, Songül frowned and said in a bitter tone, "I won't bother with her. She thinks I'm beneath her."

Songül's words dissipated in the air before reaching Yasin's ear. He was so preoccupied that he didn't even understand what she had said. For a long time, nothing was heard but the sounds of forks and spoons.

LIFE FLOWS IN ITS OWN RHYTHM. STIRRINGS, LITTLE changes in the scenery . . . Bones, flowers, cliffs . . . Everything remains distant, far from them. The goo is a wasteland of impossibilities, a rotten corner in the garden of forbidden things. With its particular pests and thorny vegetation, it enfolds Selma and disappears into eternity like a still, lifeless sea. As she flails, she realizes that she isn't in a dream, that the scene spreading before her eyes is real.

She remembered the beautiful poplars by the entrance to the village. She heard the rustling of the bright, green leaves that flourished in spring. Row after row of poplars, climbing roses, suribis, pennyroyals, beet fields . . . Would she ever see them again? She would never have guessed that she would miss the poplars more than anything else.

Her chest flinched with a bitter sigh. Her sob stuck in her throat. She was afflicted by a predicament with no way out. So, this was the great anguish she had been waiting for. She was going to make her way to death after this encounter; the union she had always longed for would take place right here.

What wouldn't she give to touch the noisy hawthorn leaves once again, to lounge on her armchair after a brief walk and read a few verses. To think that she wouldn't be able to read poetry! The tree she had been nurturing inside herself was left without water; she had been stripped of the strength to feed it the few lines it craved. A leaf from a book could unravel her knots, set her spirit free.

As she gazed at her bookshelf with sadness, she caught sight of a thin blue notebook with a worn cover. She remembered the details of that lovely afternoon with Metin, back at university. They had met at a small café.

Arriving at the café, Selma noticed that Metin had long since settled at one of the tables. He greeted her with a brilliant smile, the likes of which she had never seen before. On the table was his half-finished beer, along with this notebook before him. Random scribblings, poems . . . His own verses. She had been intrigued and asked him to read what he'd written. As he read with a bashful expression, Metin's otherwise ordinary features had been transformed by his refined intellect.

They had talked and talked, and as they talked, she realized that they could become lovers. That day, they had sailed off on an adventure to unforeseeable destinations.

Her eyes filled with tears. The lojman had also taken Metin from her. From the very start, from the day they had moved in here, it had deviously woven its web. Even if she couldn't see it being woven, the web was always there, at work. Every move she made to tear through it was absorbed by its elasticity; as if it weren't enough that it tore her from reality by covering her eyes, it grabbed her with its invisible cords, displaying its kills among the archaic, banal, suffocating relationships she longed to escape. Worse yet, it imposed upon them the tyranny of conscience, endless work, painstaking effort; it depreciated the best years of their lives, wearing them down to tattered rags. Her rage refused to subside. Even if there was a chance to break free from this nuisance, it would mean emerging from the ruins of an explosion that had destroyed her.

Where had she read that the instinct to destroy was the instinct to create, she couldn't remember.

WITH THE BABY'S AWAKENING, SHE PEELED AWAY from her thoughts. The little eyes slowly opened and closed; they were puffy, like fresh breadrolls. The baby had become so beautiful! The skin gleaming, sighs like a kitten purring, a peaceful being, unquestioning, unresisting, inside the organism that neither light nor movement could penetrate. Those soft limbs had easily adapted to the goo. Exempt from shame and envy, the baby was beyond human, beyond a fragile living creature, mixing with its surroundings like water.

It was as if the baby's entire body was nothing but a mouth, and everything about its existence gathered and exited through that soft, toothless portal. It was an active mouth, lips quivering, curving, setting in motion the rest of the baby's moist features, crowned by a bold, glistening tongue that filled an onlooker with a feeling of being caressed.

The vibrations of its face made Selma anxious; she worried that the baby might open its mouth. But she knew that sooner or later that mouth would open. The voracious mouth that didn't hesitate to attack the breast would surely have a taste of the goo. Lips, she thought, as the baby involuntarily parted them, turn into a garbage can unless they open to kiss. Yet, she had to admit that this parting of lips was as terrifying as it was sublime. The end of eternal harmony had arrived. The baby's head was upright, as if held by two marble palms. The mouth gently nuzzled the goo, an incipient personality making itself known at the hungry junction on its face.

The baby was famished, wanted to be satisfied. At last, the heart hidden in its rib cage picked up the pace. With beats forceful enough to stretch the supple skin, the cycle of the mechanism was set in motion. The esophagus stirred, helpful enzymes rushed through the walls of flesh, and the parting of lips was completed. The tongue was agile, busy. The mouth opened! The baby gasped for air as if it were being force-fed a heaping spoonful of yogurt, its eyes watered, and then it inhaled desperately. Trying to expel the goo was an impossible task. Finally, the baby swallowed it. The mouth widened with a savage, fearsome reflex, then settled on an irregular feeding pattern, clearly enjoying the taste, sucking with gusto.

THE STUNTED, DRY SHRUBS SPREADING OVER THE plains are buried in snow. Here and there, thorny red branches poke out, piercing through the whiteness. In the blustery wind, the starlings grasp the coarse thorns with their claws, rocking in their uneasy cradles. The stiff-tailed whitehead ducks, lost along the migration routes, are on the plains awaiting death; coriander, tarragon, and heather are buried under the snow in dead gardens. Lost starlings, mallard flocks whose shrill cries go unheard, weary humans, reedbeds, row after row.

Görkem looked at Selma with a pity that for the first time carried traces of compassion rather than simply disgust.

She tried to interpret the expression on Selma's face. Watching her mother dazzled her soul. This feeling was too strange. There was not a drop of kindness in Selma's false, loveless acts. And yet, Gorkem wanted to reach out to her mother, to escape this nightmare with her, even if Selma had trapped motherhood within her claws and ripped open its chest with her nails.

Despite all this, Görkem wanted to hold onto her. She would exact her revenge after they escaped the goo. For now they had to join forces and find a way out of this mess. Otherwise, they were going to perish; worse yet, they would remain suspended, motionless, right here, for eternity.

Her mother's constantly changing moods never ceased to amaze her. Until the goo had imprisoned them, the same woman had neglected her baby, basically left it to die, yet now she seemed concerned about its eating, afraid for its life.

She wanted to make eye contact with her mother. If Selma could only gather her errant reason, they could find a way out. Her eyes were so full of fear that Görkem found them even more terrifying than being imprisoned by the goo. She turned away, unable to bear her mother's bloodshot, bulging eyes any longer. Cheap paintings hanging on the wall, photographs aging in their frames, she stared at these instead. That was better.

The baby continued to gulp down the goo, insatiable. Gasping for breath every once in a while, it gorged. If this went on, its small body would crack wide open from overeating.

THE POPLARS ARE LEAFLESS, SCRAWNY, FEEBLE. LIKE abandoned corpses, alone and cursed. Witch brooms that gather darkness have closed in on the plains, huddled together beneath the bushes.

While Selma contemplated the trees, an unfamiliar melancholy settled into her chest. With their dry branches, stripped bodies, those trees were still more alive, better off than she was. Her head sagged, dangling from her neck. She had lost all hope. The door that opened onto eternity was winking at her, inviting her into her dark future. The longing she had nursed deep in her heart had vanished, falling into the bottomless sinkhole opened up by the goo.

Was no one going to help? Yasin? Didn't he wonder what had become of them? The man who knocked on their door with ridiculous excuses every single day, why wasn't he around? Couldn't he at least show up to raise the flag? But he wasn't coming. He didn't concern himself with them. Nor with the flag. Whenever she thought of him, she got irritated. His smiling naivete irked her. She couldn't stand the way he was so meek and submissive with Songül, his guileless enthusiasm toward

173

his children. And his friendship with Metin, she had been displeased from day one. He had conquered Metin by sharing his passion for soccer; he had usurped all his time. The children, Yasin, the village, everything, everyone had broken off a piece from Selma. Why had she allowed all this? She was furious with herself for having been unable to rescue Metin from all these beasts. But it was too late. Metin wasn't there, Yasin wasn't there, perhaps she herself wasn't even there. Only the goo was there. Only it was real. She was filled with regret. If only she had been more agreeable. Even if it would have been disingenuous, couldn't she have answered Yasin's questions, afforded him some small talk, not brushed him off at every opportunity? Yet she didn't! She hadn't harbored warm sentiments toward him; it hadn't even occurred to her to be nice to him. His pride must have prevailed in the end. Even that wretched character must have some personal dignity after all.

The sun was setting, the day succumbing to darkening shades of red, to winter's tedium. A muted breeze stirred the snow dust that had accumulated on the surface of the landscape, ushering them all toward a timeless void. All that would remain of this flow, these quivering images was darkness, stillness. No more vivid, lovely flowers, winding paths or refreshing breezes. An endless winter, dead poplars, Selma, enduring remorse! These were all that would remain from the destruction.

TIME HAD FORMED A CRUST AROUND ITSELF DENSE
enough to keep its movements from being detected, overwhelm-
ing Selma's grief, fragility, inscrutability. Minutes advanced
indistinctly, sensed only as an endless hum. Stifled chimes
reminded her that the progression of days, hours had stopped.

The only living thing oblivious to it all was her nameless baby.
Unaware of what engulfed it, its hungry mouth continued to
consume. She had been so stingy with her nursing that now the
baby swallowed everything, as if exacting revenge. Her motherhood was being ambushed by maggots of remorse, ruthlessly
gnawing. She yearned to reach out and hold her baby in her
arms, press its murmuring mouth to her breast, feed it on her
milk, stop it from eating any more of the goo.

Still sucking, the baby's cheeks reddened and it smiled, kick-
ing with glee. Selma's stare was filled with sadness. She had never
nursed the baby willingly. She hadn't even wanted to give birth.
Even now, she wasn't sure she truly wanted to feed it. What an
insatiable appetite it had! Its grotesque desire to eat nauseated
her. She detested needs and duties, she detested all obligations.
She saw traces of her own defeat in the lust for consumption

displayed by this fragment of herself. Passions, transgressions, red-hot desires yielding to the banality of animal instincts, life yielding to survival.

This earthworm that had managed to conceal its gluttony until now, she had given birth to it out of love for Metin. When he had whispered his desire for another child in her ear, she could not refuse him. What harm could another adorable little suckling mouth do? What burden had Görkem or Murat given them that a mere handful of a thing would add? So long as they continued leading a modest life, the children would be sources of joy, not chains around their ankles. It had all been a lie, a colossal deception. The thought of children as a financial burden hadn't even crossed her mind. She had feared they would steal her love for Metin, and her fear had been justified when the first child was born.

When Metin took on the care of Görkem and Murat, Selma had been content with her life as a reluctant mother. Still, it bothered her that Metin's attention was focused on the children rather than on her. That was the main reason they fought. Day after day, she was deprived of love's burning hunger, she longed to feel Metin's passionate hands on her skin.

Now, swallowed inside this strangeness, she noticed that her feelings had changed. The goo wasn't just impeding her movements; it was altering her feelings. To free herself from this place, she could use her children as accomplices. Previously, this would never have occurred to her. She had never felt she needed them for anything. But now, she was thinking that collaborating with Murat and Görkem could get them all out of this hell. If only she could find a way to reach them, they could tear through the goo together. But neither Görkem nor Murat knew that. Underneath it all, though, she sensed that she would not be able to break free; she had to accept that she would be unable to curb the baby's appetite, unable to extend as much as a finger.

Desperate, helpless, remorseful... She needed a higher power, a sovereign, a savior; her eyes searched for the god she had given no thought to until now. She needed to find this god, to find refuge, to dull her pain. She waited, she wept, she pleaded. The goo compelled her to invent a power to withstand it; it spurred in her the need to pray, it insisted on a god.

"Merciful God! I beg you, help me!"

"Change me! Change me, God!"

"See me, God, see me, see me, see me . . ."

"Love me, love me, love, love . . ."

"Help me!"

"Save me, my God!"

"Have mercy on me, have mercy on me, have mercy on me, have mercy on me . . ."

"Help me, please, I beg you, help me."

"Have mercy! Love me, God . . ."

"Help me! Love me! Kill me, God! Kill me, please!"

Where had she read that god was dead, she couldn't remember.

SELMA LOOKED RIDICULOUS WITH HER BULGING EYES fixed on the ceiling, Görkem thought, as she pressed her feet to the wall and pushed against it, amusing herself. This way, she could flex the goo and move a bit. If Murat were here, this game would have been much more fun. But now there was no one by her, nothing to entertain her. Her brother must be in the bedroom, all by himself, scared. She was certain that he would have felt happier with his sister at his side.

She kept to the rhythm of her game. She calculated the amount of force her toes had to exert when pushing against the wall, how far each push would thrust her, or whether inhaling or holding her breath made a difference. It occurred to her to shake herself a bit before thrusting herself forward, the way birds, before taking flight, would shake their entire bodies, starting with their rumps. So she too jiggled her whole body, and then, pressing the tips of her toes to the wall, she boosted the momentum. She remembered her mallard and a chill went down her spine. She recalled the duck in the wood stack, headless, bloated, putrid. She pictured it, down to the smallest detail. Finding the mallard had been one of those rare moments of joy when destiny persuaded her that she was loved, that she could love. Fortune had unexpectedly winked at her and offered a gift of gratitude. Those fluffy, soft feathers, those wings crowned with colors of the rainbow after a rainy morning, that brilliant tail like one of the petals of swamp lilies that sprout all across mud lakes, how enchanting, how glorious it all was. Her chest heaved, her eyes welled up with happiness. She watched her mallard, she gave it wings, she released it. Its webbed feet tucked inside its breast feathers, its head stretched forward, it was gliding inside the goo, flicking its tail. Now it hovered above Selma, now it flew by the window or over the baby's tummy, now it landed on Görkem's shoulder. As it soared, Görkem's pleasure multiplied, her breathing quickened, her chest swelled. The neon-green feathers stretching from its neck to its tail flooded the goo with light. As the mallard flapped its wings, she thrust her body, she danced, she imagined making love. Desire filled her imagination with feelings of certainty and illusion, blooming in all four directions, gushing from her irrepressibly. She felt a sweet, soft weight about her being. It fluttered, turned to dust.

WHEN HE FOUND METIN, HE WAS SHOCKED, NOT SO much that Metin was dead, but that his body had deteriorated to this extent. His arms, his face, his torso had ballooned. That human skin could turn into this! As if the body lying on the ground had consumed all the anguish of the world and cracked to death. He brushed aside the layer of snow covering the body and gazed at his friend's face. With a strange conviction, he thought he could bring him back to life. He tried to warm up the corpse. He kept rubbing its chest, its face, its arms, but then, admitting defeat, he withdrew his hands from Metin's body as if dropping two useless tools. Grabbing a lump of snow, he began to scrub his dirty palms like someone who had just committed murder. He was perplexed, with no idea what to do. Should he bring Metin to Selma, or should he run to Selma and tell her he had found Metin? He couldn't make up his mind. He was afraid.

He sat beside Metin. The deep lines on his brow had disappeared, his face was bloated, his eyes like two tiny olives stuck inside a puffy bun. One of his hands had fallen to his side, the other was on his belly. Yasin closed his eyes and tuned in to nature's vitality, listening to the sounds that reached his ear. The sound of the reedbed, the wind, the snow . . .

He felt ashamed hearing all these sounds. He couldn't accept that Metin laid there, still in the face of all this activity. If only he would open his eyes, that would be enough. Then he would see that the world turned not just for those left behind, but for him, too.

He held his friend's hand, grasped it tightly, as if pleading for help. But he couldn't bear the icy sensation in his palm for long; he loosened his fingers and closed his eyes, hoping that when he opened them again, pain would turn to joy and Metin would sit up and shake himself. He would stand before him, just a little cold, sick at most, but alive. He sighed with hope and didn't dare to take another look. The sounds that came to his ears did not belong to Metin, alas. They were the sounds of the poplars, the reedbed, the ice. Life ruled over everything else. At that moment, no one, nothing was running from death, except Yasin. The mystery of death, stripped of its riddles and secrets, stood before him, terrifying in all its starkness.

Yasin felt the weight of the world descend on his shoulders, as though he was entrusted with a responsibility for all humankind. He felt the beat of drums on top of his head, pressuring him to throw off his burden immediately. It was an accursed sensation. He had to free himself. He tried to bear the weight; exhausted, he could hardly stand.

As he turned his gaze upon the cycle of nature continuing on all around him, he waited, a plea for help in his eyes. There was no hope whatsoever. He had to resign himself to the misery that settled on his chest.

A burst of courage, and he collected himself. He looked at the road ahead and decided that he could do it, he had the strength to carry his friend. His hands had stopped trembling. As bitter saliva pooled in his mouth, he leaned to grab hold of his friend's body. The music of life could be heard in the distance. He was simply going to do what had to be done. He would take on the burden sprawled on the ground—that which was no longer human but still a piece of this world—and bring it to where it belonged.

HER STOMACH TURNED. AN ACRID LUMP SURGED IN her throat like a pack of deer tearing through the fog, trampling the earth. She looked at her children. Görkem had fallen asleep, holding Nuniş, while the baby continued slurping down the goo. She watched them, resenting the serenity in the face of her inner torment. She would rather die than live on in unbearable agony, lost in the landscape where Mount Süphan and Lake Van converged.

Something fearsome was happening to her; she was being stripped of the power to end her own suffering, denied the right to put an end to her life. Death. She wanted to breathe inside that precious thought, the only thing that was truly hers. By thinking, she could free herself, forget her captivity and calm her agony. She closed and opened her eyelids. Death. She burned with longing to savor the sensations the word caused in her. She held her breath. If only she could disappear into the contented, hermetic beauty of death. She strained to hold her breath longer but to no avail, she tried to bring her hands to her throat but couldn't.

In the end, her fears had come true. The goo had begun to conquer her spirit. Her physical body, steeped in the odor of these walls over the years, had become ordinary. A chasm had opened between her desires and her actions, and she had found her remedy by creating a second life, living in the refuge of her inner world. And this game of doubles was ending now, in just the manner she had feared. The goo was flowing into the body it held captive, with the last crumbs of her freedom eroding under the pressure of this flow, signaling the impossibility of escape. Now, perhaps for the first time, her spirit and her body were in harmony; contradictions, conflicts, and disagreements were left behind on the other side of her line of retreat.

As her mind abruptly arrived at this new notion, all the molecules, down to the last one, actively bonded together, grasped her tightly, immobilizing her. She couldn't end her torment; the goo determined even when her life would end. All her ideas, including her will to do herself harm, had been taken from her. She was trapped inside this miserable, infinite existence.

Where had she read that the one truly serious philosophical question was that of suicide, she couldn't remember.

WHEN HE LAID METIN'S CORPSE OVER HIS BACK, HIS friend slumped onto his shoulders. Taking him out of the reed-bed had been harder than anticipated. The water had completely frozen over, and with the new snow, the ice had become more slippery. He filled his lungs with the air's cold, refreshing smell. The walk wouldn't be very long, but his strength seemed like it might not measure up to Metin's weight.

He didn't want to believe that the youthful body was no longer alive. Metin was a good, honest man. He kept seeing the smile that used to light up Metin's face when they played soccer together. How happily he kicked the ball, how, every spring, he organized a tournament among the neighboring villages, the genuine affection he had for his students, Yasin could never forget these things. How could Metin die? An entire life, everything that came to be, was it all for nothing? Selma? His children? Was life this brief, this devoid of meaning?

Perhaps when he brought him home, the ice would thaw and he would return to life.

Hang in there, Metin, hang in there a little longer.

He repeated his sentences as if hallucinating. In the frigid air, his tears froze on his cheeks while his heart was burning. Mustering a last sprint, he managed to leave the reedbeds behind and climb over the hill. He turned onto the path toward the lojman. The snow crunching under his feet, the dry poplars lining his route, it seemed everything contrived to get Metin to the house. The air had warmed, the fog dissipated, the road cleared.

He was completely exhausted by the time he approached the lojman. His back hunched even more than usual under the weight of the corpse, he could barely feel his arms or legs. He had no strength to take another step; he was alone, lonely, flustered. *Run away!* the universe yelled, *And don't look back!* Somehow, part of him resisted this tempting call. Perhaps what kept him moving forward was his curiosity; he was eager to crack open the door to what needed to be seen. A warm breath escaped his lungs, but meeting the frigid air, it quickly turned into a cascade of mist and brought him to his senses. His momentary stupor interrupted, he lifted his head.

Before him stood something he had never seen before. A reckless impulse born of bewilderment made him bolt forward. He was speechless, his mind stunned, helplessly waiting for someone to yank him by the arm and bring him back to his senses. He was staring at a translucent mass that had taken the exact shape and color of the lojman. Gelatinous and heaving, with Selma and the children inside of it, hovering above the ground, stock-still. It was obvious that they were unable to move. Their faces ashen, they seemed as if asleep. As if they had been buried alive in this translucent graveyard.

Gripped by the dreadful spell of the scene before him, he forgot about Metin. The painful knot that had been lodged in his throat all day ceded to curiosity and fear.

He was filled with the desire to touch this thing he couldn't make sense of. While still holding Metin with one arm, he extended his free arm toward the object of his wonder. His body seized with anxious twitching, he was being drawn in, irresistibly. He broke out in a sweat, as excited as he was terrified. Gathering every last shred of courage to be found in the recesses of his being, he touched the alien matter. The goo responded. It swelled, it trembled and, in the blink of an eye, sucked both men in like a giant vacuum.

Yasin fainted from the shock of the experience. His limbs numbed, he had dropped Metin from his back. The goo had drawn them in with such force that they had been sucked all the way in through the living room door.

SELMA MUST HAVE REALIZED FROM THE UNDULA-tions that something was happening, because she suddenly opened her eyes. She first saw Yasin, then Metin, sprawled by the entrance. She couldn't believe her eyes. Though her mouth was shut, she let out a loud scream. She leapt toward Metin, but just like a rubber band, she was drawn back to her original position. Thrashing in place, she attempted to lunge forward once again. Her futile exertion accomplished nothing other than leaving her depleted. She lay in wait for her rage to subside and, resigning herself to her limits, calmed herself.

She looked at her beloved carefully, gazing at length at his frozen hair, his pale face that had taken on the color of the swamps, his hands, his body. She tried to imagine the movements of his lips that used to remind her of leaves rustling on trees. His face that once delighted like a painting, infinitely beautiful. How was it possible that she couldn't wrap her arms around a being so beautifully created?

She pushed at the goo with all her might. She hurled her head, she swung her hip. Her movements served only to hurt her. It seemed that nothing was left for her other than the love tearing through her body.

So, Metin hadn't been able to resist his longing for her, Selma thought. No matter how angry he had been or how far he had gone, he had returned, as always. Love had prevailed, they had overcome all the hurdles, they were together again. She was filled with happiness.

My love, you are here!

She was out of her mind with joy. She wanted to embrace her husband, to disappear in his arms, but Metin just laid there, as if asleep.

When the goo swallowed humans, it put them to sleep first, then it woke them up, she thought. She would be patient and wait for Metin to wake up. It was a precious gift just to gaze at her much-longed-for beloved.

She knew that once her husband awakened, everything would change. Metin would do whatever it took to free them from this. She shivered with a wave of joy. The nightmare was over. They would make a fresh start. This time, she would seize upon the new opportunity; she would wrap her arms around Metin, plead with him, beg for forgiveness. All their anguish would be over, they would make love at the end of it all.

She tightened her fists with hope. The goo spurted from her closed fists in bubbles, and when she opened her hands again, it flowed back in and over them. Making slight motions, she began to dance with happiness. She bobbed her body, flowers sprouted from her heart, celebrating Metin's return with her entire being.

A CALM AIR OUTSIDE. THE BRIGHTENING SKY, THE froth of the snow squalls, the unmistakable smell of the past. Secret thoughts molded into shape by contradictions, contradictions now made obvious. Then, like breath exhaled into empty air, implacable reality; the foreboding translucency revealing everything as it was.

She shook off her puzzlement over Selma's strange movements when she noticed Metin. Curious, happy, she looked at her father. He had come back, at last. Her tears, the sobs that shook her chest reverberated around her like echoes in an empty space. A blanket of happiness was being gently laid over all that had happened, and over her, too. The reunion, with a single shrug, had dispersed the dull fog shrouding her heart.

She was so joyous, so excited, that she joined in her mother's movements, dancing, swinging her hips left and right.

The nightmare was finally over. Her father had come to put an end to the turmoil she lived in, to free her from the goo. At last, she would be able to wrap her arms around her mallard, rescue Murat from the bedroom, eat to her heart's content, and play games.

The wave of triumph that caused a smile to blossom on her face spread throughout her body. She was going to tell her father all about Selma's meanness, down to the last detail. She would tell him how indifferent she had been to her children, how she didn't cook for them, how Selma didn't even lift a finger when her hand was cut and drenched in blood, all her cruelty toward the baby (even though she didn't really care much about it herself), how Selma didn't nurse it, didn't attend to its crying, and didn't even bother to name it. She was going to lean her head against her father's chest lovingly, looking into his eyes like a kitten as she listened to her mother's remorseful pleas. She was not ever going to forgive Selma.

Her father had returned just in time to put an end to evil, like a true hero! He was going to destroy Selma, the guardian of darkness, and rescue his daughter, the one who deserved life and beauty.

METIN WAS SO BEAUTIFUL. SUNLIGHT TOUCHING HIS skin, the features of his face, his vulnerable body generously presenting itself for her gaze. In stillness, the delicate craftsmanship of his lips, his nose, his chin became all the more evident, the measured curves all the more remarkable.

All of her attachment to Metin, her longing, her maddening passion had not been in vain. She could no longer endure the endless, draining wait. Hours, days seemed to pass, but Metin didn't wake up, the dream didn't end, the goo didn't disappear. Waiting for Metin to awaken was more agonizing than waiting to be released from the goo in his absence.

The weariness gnawing at her heart grew stronger. She writhed with the torment of being unable to touch her beloved. Love was flesh finding its voice, bodies talking to each other, a communion of the senses, desiring, burning, a wildfire. All that pious, sacred, spiritual blather meant nothing to her. She wanted her skin, thirsty for love, to be washed in Metin's sweat, cleansed in his elixir, their cries of pleasure uniting as one, demolishing the village, the lojman, and the children in its thundering reverberations.

The questions swarming her mind were unbearable. Had the goo done something to him? Had it sent him into shock by sucking him in so instantly; had he not been able to withstand the force, poor man? But was Metin really too feeble to endure such a jolt? The goo couldn't have defeated him. The Metin she knew wouldn't even be touched by such small troubles.

She glanced at Yasin, whose eyelids twitched every now and then; she expected him to wake up and talk to her. How had they gotten there, where had he met Metin, what had Metin told him; she wanted to find out everything.

Yasin! Yasin!

Yasin, wake up! Wake up, Yasin!

What did Metin tell you? Did he miss me?

Yasin, wake up! Wake up! Come on now, wake up!

Forgive me, forgive me, Yasin.

Wake up, Yasin, forgive me.

What did he tell you? Did he miss me?

Forgive me, Yasin, make a sound, talk to me, save me.

Selma became more confused. Yasin didn't speak. Was he doing this on purpose? Did he want to drive her crazy by ignoring her? Her helplessness enraged her. She hurled expletives at Yasin. She ordered him to answer her questions. She may as well have been shouting at a wall.

She could hear her own spirit being crushed. Like a spectator, she watched despair vanquishing her. Her mind crashed into looming cliffs, she ruminated on random things, unhinged, she spewed whatever thoughts came to her mind, one after another.

The beast in me, he spurred on.

From deer's milk I made bread. Come, take me already.

What did he say, Yasin? Did he miss me?

Kill me, Yasin! Love, love!

He came, he left, never looked back. You still out there?

Love me, love! Kill me, dear God! Change me, love me!

The echoes clung to her lips like oversalted morsels; they shook the goo in silent tremors.

THE BABY GREW BIG AND RUDDY. CHEEKS PUFFED UP, arms and legs ballooning in rolls of fat, chin multiplied in pudgy waves. Playful fingers wiggled, moving over its immense belly; hints of delight rippled across its face.

Selma saw it wolf down Nuniş along with the goo. She anxiously observed the insatiable appetite of this body that was expanding as she watched. The baby was a disturbing sight, but she couldn't turn away. Its toothless, spongy mouth was irresistible. Her hair stood on end every time the mouth opened and closed, reckless, like a pack of jackals that materialize to clean up after a kill. Its relentless gorging had gone beyond human capacity. Maybe there was no such thing as being human, it was an impossibility. The notion had been invented, and it was only later that some value had been assigned to it. Meaning, sense, the sacred, all lost their value in this torrent, tumbling into emptiness.

Her feelings about her baby warped, she didn't know what to feel, how to describe it, she was helpless. If someone were to ask whose child this creature was, she wouldn't even be able to reply. A bastard birthed by the lojman, she thought to herself, a monstrosity suckled on the goo, nothing more. Certainly not mine or Metin's.

Would it all have turned out the same had they given it a name, she wondered? Did humans mutate into such monsters when they went unnamed? Was that why, the moment a baby was born, better yet, while it was still in its mother's womb, they rushed to find a name for it? So that it could be distinguished from ravenous animals, from dark beasts?

How well the idle greed that ruled the stomach of this fearsome monster matched its namelessness. She wracked her brain; what could one call this child? What kind of a name could she choose? She'd had a hard enough time with the other children. That's why others had taken care of that intimate task. Had she been satisfied by their choices? No! Görkem was named by Metin's childhood friend. Just because they couldn't say no to him, and Görkem's name never suited her; it stuck to her like a disgusting, insect-shaped brooch pinned on an elegant gown. She had never seen Murat as her own flesh and blood, perhaps because of his name. The moment when Metin's sister said, "Let's name the baby Murat," she'd felt like they were adopting Murat from another family, and instead of fighting that feeling, she had cultivated no warm affection toward her second child either.

Erratic sentences were beginning to crowd her mind. Metin not waking up, Yasin stubbornly refusing to make a sound, it rattled her patience.

Metin, wake up, wake up, my love! she raised her voice once more. Let's go away, let's get away from this nameless maggot and the other pests!

Kill me Metin, come on, wake up!

Yasin, wake Metin up, you filth! Speak! Did he miss me? Did he tell you anything?

Yasin, kill me, wake Metin up, take us out of here.

Forgive me! Yasin, love me!

THE MOUTH OPENS, SUCKS IN THE GOO, THE CHEEKS
swell. The mouth closes, a moment's pause, the lips get back
to work. As if this is how one withstands a strange agony. The
side table, the chair, the bookshelf . . . Infinity widens, its active,
interdependent reality makes its presence known as an inscrutable annihilation.

Selma was the only one to blame for the baby's insatiable
appetite. Had she fed it properly, cared for it, maybe it wouldn't
have turned into such a greedy beast. She cared about nothing,
except reading those old, awful books day in day out. Didn't the
books ever talk about how to be a good mother? Or did she
lack the intellect to understand what she read? There she was,
perched in her corner like an owl, indulging her unhinged personality, watching the monster she had created with total indifference. Shut this baby's mouth, at least do that much, Selma!

What a sad state she was in! Tired, spent, starved for love.
But who wasn't starved for love! If only, for a day, even for a brief
moment, she had experienced that feeling, if only she had been
loved, kissed, caressed, spoiled, everything could have turned
out differently. Her emotions were a tangled mess. At times, she

pitied her mother, at others, she detested her. A sledgehammer that kept hitting her on the head, banging her down and down, inflaming her malevolence. As the baby approached with its enormous suction power, she wasn't sure what to do.

The mouth was so large that every time it opened, she could easily see the uvula, dangling like a giant wad of dough. Aghast, she watched, eyes fixed on the mouth, the tiny lip movements, the stretched skin. It gorged without stopping, without pausing for breath, consuming as it approached. She shut her eyes, clenched her fists, waiting to die in that gruesomeness.

THAT SHAPELESS, GUZZLING, ALL-CONSUMING MOUTH
was an unrelenting annihilator; attacking the material form of
things, swallowing and digesting them, absorbing them in its
metabolism, creating absences in its wake—the imprints left on
the floor by the legs of a table no longer there, the memory of
a few verses thrown from a dislodged bookshelf—the creature
that had been steadily closing in on Görkem made a lumber-
ing, ungainly move and turned in the direction of Selma. Selma,
who bore her motherhood like a painful hump on her back.

Calmly, she turned her eyes away from the baby; there was
nothing left to see. Death, no longer a mere possibility, took on
form, a body, it expanded, it surrounded. Görkem was gripped
by a fear of being left motherless.

The goo melted into Selma's skin, the mouth grinned vora-
ciously, it advanced as if pouncing on a nipple. Alluring, gleaming, immense. Fear and terror lost their meaning, each turning
into a dead word.

Watching Selma's body being swallowed (first my legs I didn't
feel much at first haven't been walking haven't needed them
much walking gets you nowhere step after step treading the same

old paths you walk a thousand roads and realize you've barely walked that's why you don't feel them your toes your soles the splayed bones the joints they don't belong to you the world's not good for walking what's it good for anyway it's biting me with its tiny teeth that haven't pierced through the gums tearing little bits of my flesh its mouth is so beautiful looks a bit like mine oh I swoon every time I see its mouth I shiver as if an ice cube is sliding down my back cooling me all that flows into me from that little mouth bliss arousal emptying I let it eat me wrapped by an old feeling from the days when I kissed Metin his mouth so many times the first time was when I invited him home we were alone he was afraid he started to recite poems I hushed him why do mouths keep talking why do they never stop I kissed him then and never let go of those lips I followed him everywhere he went I tailed him I couldn't live without him would've dried and withered but this mouth is it mine is it tired of me and depleting me if only it stayed away from my hands not dig its teeth into my hands when it's done devouring my hands then it's my calves my belly I bet watching me writhe in pain whets its appetite I realize my hands whetted its appetite somehow but how I'd touch myself I need my hands legs are filthy hands give joy give bliss reach deep breasts are also filthy without Metin I don't want them to feed anyone the natural functions of the organs disgust me it can eat it all it's moving up soon there'll be nothing left of me it's panting it's out of breath I watch my mouth my nose being sucked in fluids mucus usurped from my windpipe it hurts a little a bearable sort of hurt it's done with my hands my throat my windpipe is next it shuts its eyes as if swooning it takes my mouth in its mouth biting my lips with

its tiny teeth that haven't pierced the gums I won't get to kiss
Metin ever again I kept fighting you your laughter oh how you'd
lean drowsily into my chest I'd press you into my flesh as if to
smother you I'd muss up your face your hair pull out a few tufts
and stick them on your sweaty nape we'd flirt and caress we'd
seethe and stew we were soft as soft balms squeezed from their
tubes some nights you'd lie face down next to me the crinkled
skin around your eyes your mouth thirsty for blood I'd kiss your
mouth you'd suck on my chin wrap your arms around me a spin-
dly vine cut at the roots I was afraid I'd go mad while loving you
a god stood next to us who didn't belong to us who disallowed
embracing who forbade carnal passions we took it everywhere
stuck it in every hole that belonged to us it became exalted holy
ugh finish already I'm tired tired of those thoughts that did
me no good those fantasies that didn't even crack open a door
didn't point to a way out thoughts just thoughts and nothing
more reason is our flaw all this ridding ourselves from excesses
all this understanding what defies understanding why doesn't it
hurry up and finish I hate it come already free this mind liber-
ate me it's loosening are we at the end is it over this rotting this
putrefaction obligations questions it's devouring me it's up to
my eyes they are no more nor is Metin and nor am I but had I
ever been was I ever here of course I was Metin knows we are
dying together what joy no more desires either nor passions no
more wildfires we are exactly where we need to be we can die
they couldn't take this from us what joy doesmyhairstillsmell
and now my head it devoured my mouth am I ugly no no Metin
come comecaressmecomeloveme killthekidskillYasin dontgivein
willpowerisourdevil theresacorpse acorpsetobury) Görkem

relived Teacher Mahir's memory, his lips, his fingers that never once traveled across her skin.

She knew it, she wasn't inside a nightmare. Or, if this was a nightmare, it hadn't just begun. The goo had been there all along; smeared on the gray walls, the flag poles, mixed in the coal sheds, the darkness, the light, the desires, the fears, the mallard corpses, seeping into their thoughts, it had been right by their side everywhere, in what they did, what they couldn't do, what they couldn't imagine doing.

Murmuring, the baby advances, laughs, giggles, waves its blubbery arms. There's no more Selma! Desire accompanies the mouth, it doesn't end, it won't be fulfilled, it won't be sated. The emptiness left from Selma joins the emptiness of everything and everyone else. Metin, Murat, Yasin . . . The baby pauses to catch its breath beside Görkem; their eyes meet. A spark of joy radiates from Görkem's gaze, a gaze that's content to behold the world for the last time, wondering how it endured life all this time. Gently, she closes her eyes, she trembles, presents herself to the soft, doughy lips. The emptiness left from her is just like her mother's, a pinch that shrinks and shrinks into a smooth, shallow spot. She gets caught by her legs, her arms, thrill rises from her abdomen to her neck alongside a tingling, titillating pain. She lets go to unite with Teacher Mahir, her one and only love, and presents her body to her brother for devouring.

THE GOO WAS COMPLETELY SPENT, THE SCHOOL building next to the lojman, and the village, all had been consumed. Perplexed, the baby looked about, took a deep breath, its chest expanding, contracting. With pudgy steps it toddled around in the snow.

It was alone on the immense plains. The snow had subsided, but the landscape that opened into the dark and all-encompassing eternity was still there with all its gloom. No sound was heard except the rustling of the wind. Frost was in the air; it was freezing cold. The mallards had forsaken the outline of Lake Van. Winter had covered the Erciş Plateau and imposed its sovereignity by destroying every small spark of life. The poplar trees had dried up, the beet fields were forgotten beneath the whiteness.

Winter exacted a profound and absolute resignation. Just as it had put the whole plateau to eternal sleep, it would put the baby to sleep, cradling it in its omnipresence and giving it peace, putting an end to its exertion, freeing it at last from both its voracious appetite and its inexhaustible hunger.

The baby stumbled, a colossal body grown unwieldy, the blood's rhythm surrendering to the flow of nature. The giant eyelids closed over the bloodshot eyes, the entire body slumped into the snow, trusting itself to winter's murmur like succumbing to a lullaby from a warm voice, swaying left and right, then falling into an eternal slumber as the snowflakes, flickering, tremulous, covered it with their blanket. With its newborn's mouth, full cheeks, soft, downy belly, the baby belonged to nature now. The way everything belongs to nature, malicious and beautiful.